DANCE
of the
Snow Dragon

DANCE
of the
Snow Dragon

Eileen Kernaghan

Thistledown Press Ltd.

Canadian Cataloguing in Publication Data
Kernaghan, Eileen
Dance of the snow dragon
ISBN 1-895449-41-3
I. Title.
PS8571.E695D3 1995 C813'.54 C95-920052-5
PR9199.3.D469D3 1995

Book design by A.M. Forrie
Cover art by Rand Walsh
Set in 11pt New Baskerville by
Thistledown Press

Printed and bound in Canada by
Webcom Printing Ltd.
Scarborough, Ontario

Thistledown Press Ltd.
663 Main Street
Saskatoon, Saskatchewan
S7H 0J8

This book has been published with the assistance of
The Canada Council and the Saskatchewan Arts Board.

This one is for Michael

We shall not cease from exploration . . .
T.S. Eliot

Special thanks to Mary Choo, who first told me about the Bhutanese dancers. As well, I am indebted to Madame Alexandra David-Neel, Katie Hickman, Sue Kernaghan, and other Himalayan travellers whose accounts provided background material and inspiration.

CONTENTS

No one can know whether the world is fantastic or real, or whether there is a difference between dreaming and living.

Jorge Luis Borges

PROLOGUE

One son from every family: that was the time-honoured law of Druk-yul. When Sangay Tenzing was five, and his brother Norbu was two, a party of astrologer monks from the distant White Leopard Monastery arrived in their village.

The village was small and isolated — a few wood and stone houses clustered in a steep-walled northern valley. That morning, when the Lamas approached along the river road in their garnet-coloured robes and tall red hats, word spread quickly. All the aunts and uncles, cousins and neighbours trooped in from the fields to gather in the muddy courtyard of Sangay's house.

The monks and Sangay's parents exchanged white ceremonial scarves. Gongs and trumpets sounded. Prayer-wheels turned with a clamour of small bells. All day the astrologer monks crouched over their horoscope charts, and finally the choice was made.

"I thought they would choose little Norbu," said Sangay's mother Yeshe Kunley. "It is not reasonable, when we have only two sons, to take the eldest. How shall we we manage without Sangay to mind the yaks?"

"Be still," said Sangay's father, embarrassed. "They will hear you." But Yeshe Kunley was a forthright woman, determined to speak her mind.

"He will be so far away, my little Sangay. How shall I be able to visit him? Why can he not go to the monastery in our own valley, where he has cousins to look out for him?"

Her brother Jigme Kunzang, who was the village lay-priest, said, "Think of the honour, Yeshe Kunley. To have a son at the White Leopard Dzong! Did I not always say that Sangay was destined for great things? You remember how many lucky signs were observed at his birth? And now these Learned Ones have travelled for days to seek him out — surely they must have heard rumours of an extraordinary child in our midst."

Yeshe Kunley gazed sadly at her firstborn. In the midst of all the commotion — the clash of cymbals and booming of drums, the mantra-drone and the villagers' excited chatter — he was calmly ringing a ritual bell that one of the monks had given him. He was a sturdy child, strong-boned and tall for his age, but with little, as far as she could tell, to set him apart from other children. Although . . . Yeshe thought of that look he sometimes wore. She had noticed it, and told Jigme Kunzang about it, the first day she held Sangay in her arms. It was the look of one who saw the world through his third, invisible eye, perceiving what others could not.

"He is a dreamer, if that's what you mean," she told her brother. "When he has that far-off look and I ask him what he sees, he tells me, 'Dances'. Now I ask you, Jigme Kunzang, how will he attend to his studies, when he is forever making up dances in his head?"

As for Sangay, he was too young to understand that on this day the pattern of his life had been decided. He knew only that for a while, to his surprise, he had been the centre of everyone's attention; and that after the chanting faded, the white scarves of farewell had been exchanged and the Lamas went away, his mother wept.

Book One

The White Leopard
Dzong

THE CHOSEN ONE

Good morning, Holy One," said Sangay. Precious Cloud lowered her shaggy head so he could scratch behind her ears. She was immense, sweet-tempered, white as milk — a creature favoured by the gods.

Tethered next to the great white yak was Sangay's special favourite, Spring Flower. She had just given birth, and Sangay squatted to look at the new calf. Half-hidden in long, soft hair, it was suckling furiously. Spring Flower shied at Sangay's touch, tossing her head and dragging at her rope. She was young and skittish; not yet accustomed to motherhood. Sangay clicked his tongue in a comforting way and dropped a pinch of juniper incense into the fire, to drive away the night-demons.

He spread his hands over the flames. It was bitter cold this morning, in the shadow of the Goddess's mountain. The wind tasted of snow. He finished another cup of butter-tea, waiting for the first thin rays of the sun to reach the valley and burn away the mists. When he knew that he could delay no longer, he untethered his grunting, moaning, spitting charges, and herded them onto the steep path to the yak-pastures.

On a level patch of ground part way up the mountain was a wayside shrine, a *chorten*. Sangay walked three times round it, muttering a prayer:

Salutation to the Buddha.
In the language of the gods and the demi-gods,
in the language of demons and of men
in all the languages that exist
I proclaim the Doctrine . . .

Then — as on every other morning — he turned to look down into the valley. Streamers of mist still hung in the high air, like tattered prayer-flags. A long way below, he could see the wind-rippled gold of buckwheat fields; a wide green band of meadow; and then a huddle of steep, sungilt roofs. In the centre of the village, where that thread of smoke curled up, was his own house. By now his father would have left for the fields, while his brother Norbu still dawdled by the fire. His mother would be stirring the stew-cauldron, or spinning yarn with the new girl-baby Llamo swaddled on her back.

It was time to move on. The yaks stood contentedly enough, twitching their bushy tails and grinding their teeth; but now that Sangay had stopped climbing, he felt the deep chill in the air. He whistled and tossed a handful of stones at the yaks to urge them forward.

It was early still when he reached the prayer-wall at the top of the path. The old stones were cracked and lichened, the mantra so faded that even a monk would have to guess at what it had once said. Sangay turned, as he had been taught, to the four directions of the world, and to the top and bottom of the sky. "May all things be happy," he said into the icy wind.

Beyond the wall his aunt Dorjee, the village sorceress, crouched among some boulders picking herbs. Every few days she came to this high pasture to gather materials for her spells and healing potions; today she had brought her two small granddaughters with her.

The older girl, Dechen, had already caught sight of Sangay. She raced across the pasture, followed at a distance by small, moon-faced Nima, who wailed because her stocky legs could not keep up.

Dechen threw herself down on the grass, panting. Her plain, solemn face was flushed by the cold.

"Grandmother says it is tomorrow you must leave."

Sangay nodded.

"Are you frightened, cousin?"

"Why should I be frightened? What place could be safer than the Great Dzong?"

Of course he was frightened — who would not be? But he could not give this girl-cousin the satisfaction of knowing it.

"Think of this, Dechen," he said. "When the snows come, when you lie by your hearthside listening to the wolves howl, I will be sleeping on a soft rug inside the fortress walls."

"You are teasing me, Sangay Tenzing. You always tease me. You know I would rather die than leave my family and go to live among strangers."

"You are younger than me. And anyway you are a girl." He spoke with a boldness that went no deeper than his smile.

Dechen turned her head and called out sharply to Nima who, heedless as always, was tottering after a yak calf, perilously near the cliff-top. Then, glancing slyly at Sangay, she said, "It is a long way to the Valley of the Great Dzong. There will be wild beasts, and wood-demons . . ."

"And a whole company of monks to protect me with their prayers."

"If I were you," persisted Dechen, "I would not go. I would run away into the forest and hide in a cave. My grandmother would bring me food, and teach me sorcery. Then when I was a grown woman I would come back to the village, and they would have to let me stay."

Sangay grinned at her, pleased that he was to have the last word. "And do you think they would choose you to be a monk?"

"There are woman monks," said Dechen, glowering. "Everybody knows that."

"But not such timid ones as you," said Sangay, and howled with laughter when she shook her fist at him.

His eighth birthday had seemed a long way in the future, when the Lamas first came to the village. He had been five then — old enough to enter the monastery, in spite of his mother's protests. But the monks, who were not unreasonable men, had agreed that Sangay could remain at home for three more years. By then the baby Norbu would be grown, and could take his brother's place as yak-herd.

Sangay sighed, and settled his back against a rock. After today, everything would be different. Spring Flower's calf would grow up, and he would not be here to see it. Would Norbu remember to braid flowers in Precious Cloud's tail on feast-days?

Rummaging in the waist-fold of his *kho*, he pulled out some buckwheat cakes and a string of cheeses. Dorjee and the children had moved off to the far end of the pasture. The air was hazy still; the small figures of his girl-cousins, playing with the calves among the juniper-scrub, seemed vague as ghosts. Cloud-spirits, thought Sangay, sleepily, remembering stories of the Sky-Travellers who, dancing between earth and heaven, show us the pathway to a higher plane. Through half-closed eyes he saw whole troupes of ghostly figures drifting, circling, whirling, bounding, turning enormous cartwheels in the air. It was a game he often played, on these long days in the high pasture. Everything he could see that moved — prayer-flags, wind-tossed azalea bushes, scudding clouds, yak calves frisking in the sun — became part of a vast and complex temple-dance, that swept across the high meadows and the mountain-tops, and into the wide air beyond.

THE JOURNEY BEGINS

Sangay woke next morning to familiar sounds and smells: the crackle of the hearth, dogs barking, the sour odour of fermenting maize. He shivered and rolled nearer the fire. Then he remembered, with a sudden racing of his heart, that this was not a day like any other.

His mother was bending over him. In the smoky half-light her face looked tired and sad. As he sat up she put a steaming cup into his hand.

"Drink your tea, my son," she whispered. "You will need its warmth on your long journey."

She was dressed as for a feast-day in her best *kira* and her new red jerkin. Necklaces of amber, turquoise and coral clattered softly as she moved. Her hands in the firelight gleamed with silver.

Sangay put on the clean new *kho* his mother had made for him from red and blue and green striped cloth, hitching it up and belting it tightly so that the loose fabric fell in a neat waist-fold.

Outside, in the raw morning, six monks were waiting. Five had the long sober faces of officials; the sixth was young, round-cheeked, cheerful-looking. His dark eyes smiled at Sangay.

There were parting gifts: a red-lacquered bowl made of rhododendron wood, a long-bladed knife, some buckwheat cakes, a string of small hard cheeses. Sangay tucked them into the fold of his *kho*.

He stood on the painted porch, staring at objects so familiar that he had never thought to examine them before. He looked at a bunch of dried chilis hanging from a beam; a basket of maize; his mother's loom.

I may never set eyes on this house again, he thought; his throat hurt, but he knew he must not weep before the monks.

His mother and father walked with him as far as the *chorten* at the village-edge, where the rest of the people had already gathered. His mother carried little Llamo in her arms. The baby, fretful with her first tooth, was wailing, and Sangay's mother herself seemed on the verge of tears.

The village boundary was marked out with twigs and bunches of flowers. Bright rugs covered the ground; a fire was burning, and as soon as the monastery party appeared, cups of butter-tea were handed round. The monks and Sangay's parents exchanged white ceremonial scarves. His mother hugged Sangay hard against her breast. Then it was time to go.

The young monk walked beside Sangay. "You must not look so downcast," he said. "Think of your good fortune in being chosen."

Sangay attempted a smile. "I am not downcast," he said, hoarse-voiced.

The young monk said, "I went away from my village to the Dzong when I was much younger than you. It was hard, at first, and I missed my family. But the Dzong is a fine place, and anyway, you will be much too busy to grieve."

Sangay did not reply. After a time the monk went on, "The White Leopard Dzong is famous for its dancing. Do you like to dance?"

For the first time Sangay noticed how gracefully this young man walked, how he seemed to spring along the path like a big sleek cat. Every part of him appeared to fit precisely with every other part. His hands moved like the wings of birds, speaking with a voice of their own.

Ruefully, Sangay considered his own large hands and feet, his long ungainly limbs. "I am far too clumsy," he replied.

"Perhaps. To each of us, his own gift. You are tall for your age, and you look strong — maybe you will be an archer. Well, that is not for you nor I, but for the Abbot to decide."

Behind them, the villagers were still waving scarves and banners, and shouting out farewells. Long after the village fields were out of sight, Sangay imagined that he could hear those faint cries.

The pine forest closed around them. For the first part of the way the journey was pleasant enough. Morning sunlight slanted through the high branches; the ground was carpeted with moss and violets. Soon, though, the sunlight vanished and the trail rose steeply. Now ferns and creepers choked their path, and the trees were shrouded in long grey curtains of old man's beard. Where the shadows were deepest, toadstools grew like strange pale flowers. This was the haunted twilight wood of fireside tales, where ghosts and demons lurked, and all manner of dangerous beasts prowled the tangled underbrush. Sangay kept carefully to the narrow track, close at the young monk's heels.

They climbed higher, through a flowering forest of giant pink and scarlet rhododendrons, and then at last they had reached the prayer-wall at the top of the pass. The far side of the mountain, ridge upon ridge of blue-black forest, fell away below them.

Looking down, Sangay could see no sign of houses, or tents, or yak herds. He and the six monks seemed to be the only living creatures under that huge sky, alone in a silent world of mist and pines.

They followed the narrow mountain paths over hanging bridges of bamboo, up stairways carved in living rock. Every pass was crowned with a lichened, weathered pile of mani-stones, each with its small serene inscription, *Om mani padme hum* — "Behold, the Jewel in the Lotus" — the ancient letters faint and spidery as a message from the land of ghosts.

Towards evening they came down into a sunny hollow in the hills. In this sheltered place, set on a rise of ground and surrounded by cypresses and sandalwood, rose the white stone walls of a monastery. Its gilded roofs, dazzling in the slanted light, looked to Sangay as though they were on fire.

Inside the monastery gates was a cobbled courtyard, from the centre of which rose a carved and painted tower, with doorways opening beyond. From somewhere nearby came the soft clash of cymbals, the pulse of drums.

The monks welcomed them as honoured guests, gave them butter-tea and rice, and when they had eaten invited them to visit the three temples for which this monastery was renowned.

Sangay kept lagging behind the others as they proceeded from room to room. There were so many new things to see and marvel at. How amazed Dechen would be, if only he could tell her! In the first temple, huge frescoes in glowing colours showed smiling saints,

Buddhas and Bodhisattvas floating serenely on
their lotus thrones. In the second temple, an
enormous gold and scarlet dragon looped and
twisted across the walls. In the flickering light
of the butter-lamps it seemed to flash its eyes
and snap its jaws. It was the great dragon of
Druk-yul, said the young monk Wanjur, nudging Sangay onward — the dragon of the snows
whose voice rang out across the mountain
peaks like thunder.

The six monks settled themselves before the
shrine to say a mantra. All around them the
sound of chanting rose and fell like a soft wind.
The air was filled with a sweet, smoky fragrance.
Sangay had not imagined that so astonishing a
place could exist in the ordinary world of men.

"And yet," said Wanjur, afterwards, "this is
only a little out-of-the-way monastery. You must
not imagine you have seen anything wonderful,
until you have beheld the White Leopard
Dzong."

The third temple was dedicated to the Pro-
tective Gods of the Valley. Here, the walls were
covered with old weapons and rhinoceros skin
shields. In the centre of the shrine was a mandala fashioned from ritual dagger-nails. These,

Wanjur whispered to Sangay, were the same nails with which the ancient demon-gods of Druk-yul had been fastened to the ground, so that they might never again escape to torment humankind.

That night Sangay slept in a small smoky room on the upper floor. He should have slept long and dreamlessly, in such a holy place. And yet his rest was troubled by visions. Most of these he had forgotten within moments of opening his eyes; but one dream was to stay with him for many days. He had seen a nightmare image of a demoness, vast as the land of Druk-yul itself, and he was pounding daggernails through the coils of her writhing serpenthair, through her huge black flailing feet and clawing hands. When the last nail was driven, that immense and hideous bulk stretched harmlessly from the southern foothills of Druk-yul to the jagged snowpeaks of the north; and everywhere there was singing and rejoicing. Yet waking in his moment of triumph, still Sangay was troubled by what he had seen.

Danger on the Road

All next morning they threaded their way across the hills. Each thickly wooded slope seemed steeper than the last. On one side of the narrow track rose walls of stone, light-drenched and glittering with waterfalls; on the other side, the ground dropped away into sunless gorges, choked with bamboo and lichen-covered trees.

Near the top of a high pass, they met a party of women in nun's garments, resting beside the trail. These were pilgrims bound for the Holy Mountain, the abode of the Goddess Jo-mo lHari, which lay an unimaginable distance to the west on the border of Khang-yul, Land of Snows. Yet they had no tents, no pack-horses, no provisions — not so much as a brick of tea to share among them, as far as Sangay could tell. Some of the women were weeping; all looked ragged and travel-weary.

"Be careful," one of the pilgrims warned the monks. "There is a band of brigands lurking just beyond the pass. They stopped us on the road and robbed us of all our food and gold. Now our journey will be a hard one, for in these mountains there are few villages or monasteries where we can beg for shelter."

"What will we do?" Sangay whispered to Wanjur.

"What can we do? We cannot turn back, so we must go on." So saying, Wanjur unrolled his pack, lifting out a folding travel-bow and a sheaf of arrows.

As the monks neared the summit of the pass and prepared to make their ritual circuit of the *chorten*, the Chief Monk turned for a moment, glancing first at Sangay, and then at Wanjur. It was as though some unspoken message had passed between the two men.

"Get back," said Wanjur to Sangay, gesturing with his chin. "There, behind those rocks — stay there, and do not move until I tell you."

Sangay scuttled out of sight, as he was bid. But now he could not see what was happening on the road. What he needed was a spy-hole. He found a clump of heather growing in a chink between two boulders and tugged at it with both hands until it came free, roots and all. When he put one eye to the opening, he had a clear view of the path.

An instant later, five tall, scowling men came up over the crest of the hill. They wore the skins of animals over their coarse loose-sleeved shirts, and carried swords and spears. Standing shoulder to shoulder, they completely blocked the narrow track.

"Give us a present, Honourable Sirs," said one of the strangers. He spoke politely enough, and Sangay wondered if this might be some odd custom of the country, to demand a gift from every wayfarer. But then he saw that the Chief Monk's hand was resting on the hilt of the short-sword thrust through his belt, and that Wanjur had unobtrusively strung his bow and was fitting arrow to nock.

"A present, if you please," the man repeated, still speaking as courteously as if he

were asking some small favour of the monks —
a blessing, or a soothsaying.

"We have nothing to spare," the Chief
Monk told him, and Sangay observed that the
monk's sword had leaped suddenly into his
hand.

"Make way," he heard the Chief Monk say
quietly. "Step aside, or it will be the worse for
you."

At that threat, so mildly spoken, the bandit
grinned. "And how will it be the worse for us,
when we have your gold, which you will give to
us because you are virtuous and generous-
hearted monks?"

The brigands, brandishing their weapons,
made a wall through which no escape seemed
possible. There was sheer rock on one side of
the path, on the other a yawning gulf of air.

The Chief Monk said, "We are Superior
Monks of the White Leopard Dzong, which
governs the whole of this region. Lay a hand on
any one of us, and the Dzongda's warriors will
have your skulls for drinking bowls."

There was a moment's silence, and then the
leader of the brigands said, "There is a mountain or two yet, between here and the White

Leopard Dzong. Are the Dzongda's warriors demons, that they can cross mountains quick enough to catch us?"

For reply, the Chief Monk threw his arms into the air and began to invoke the names of the Fifty-Eight Wrathful Gods, those fearsome animal-headed apparitions which inhabit the dark regions of the afterworld.

"You had better be aware," said Wanjur, raising his voice to be heard over the Chief Monk's wailing, "that this Holy One is a famous *naljorpa* sorcerer, trained in the arts of the *ningma-ningma*, the most ancient of ancients, in Khang-yul, Land of Snows. By the power of his magic he keeps a Malevolent and Invisible One chained over there in that pile of rocks. In fact, we have just now renewed the binding spell, to ensure that the creature will not escape."

The Chief Monk continued to intone his awful syllables. The brigands were beginning to look uncertain. Playing for time, their leader scratched thoughtfully under his hat. One of the robbers, the smallest and youngest, took a step backward, half-concealing himself behind a larger comrade.

"Listen," Wanjur shouted suddenly. "Can you not hear him, clawing and scrabbling among the rocks? The prayers of the Holy One have woken him, and he is restless. There, now he is rattling his chains, and scraping them against the stones."

From his hiding place, Sangay watched and listened. He recognized the game that the monks were playing — and he understood the part that he was to take in it. It was the kind of trick he had delighted in playing on Dechen, when she pestered him to share his food with her. But this time it was not a few cheeses on a string that were at stake. They were playing for their lives.

He gathered up a handful of loose stones and tossed them as high as he could so that they scattered on the path at the brigand's feet. He had no chains to rattle, so he threw back his head and began, by turns, to howl, and shriek, and groan.

Peering through his hole in the rocks, he saw stark terror on the faces of the robbers; delighted, he redoubled his efforts. He cried out in the wolf's voice, and in the leopard's. With his hands to his mouth he produced the shrill whine of the mountain wind, the moan of temple-horns, the grunting of yaks, the ominous bellow of funeral conches.

The monks were slowly advancing, swords in hands. Wanjur let fly a well-placed arrow which tore the robber-chief's fur-trimmed cap from his head without disturbing one hair of his scalp. The robber reached up, astonished, to touch the place where his hat had been. As he raised his arm a second arrow, hard on the first, pierced the loose fabric of his sleeve and pinned it to the trunk of a windfall tree that leaned half-uprooted across the path.

The brigand howled with rage and dragged at the shaft with his free hand. A third arrow hissed, and pinned that sleeve to the tree as well. There he hung like a drying yak-skin, utterly helpless, his face ash-grey with fear.

Sangay held his breath, forgetting to howl, as he waited for the fourth arrow to sing its way to the brigand's heart. The other robbers, meanwhile, had seized the opportunity to flee back down the trail, abandoning their chief to whatever fate the gods might have in store for him.

But Wanjur had lowered his bow. "Come
out, Sangay," he said.

Obediently, Sangay crept out from behind
the rocks.

"Well done, demon," said Wanjur, and he
laughed as he slung his bow across his back.

The monks, short-swords in belts, piously
chanting, made their circuit of the *chorten.* And
then they went on down the mountainside.
Behind them they could hear the robber curs-
ing horribly as he struggled, without much
success, to tear loose the tough fabric of his
sleeve.

THE *MANIP'S* TALE

Late in the day it began to rain — a cold drizzle that soaked the shoulders of Sangay's *kho* and worked its way down the back of his neck. Wretched but uncomplaining, he trudged behind Wanjur, bare feet squelching in the mud. Then, as the light faded, mist rolled in. Now all that Sangay could see of the monks were vague grey shapes creeping ghostlike along the path ahead.

Night was fast approaching, and they began to watch for a yak-hut or a cave where they could take shelter. Finally, to their relief, the path levelled and turned downward; faintly through the mist they heard the clatter of yak-bells and the moan of temple-horns.

They spent that night in the village headman's house — a three-storied building of
stone, mud-plaster and elaborately painted
wood, which seemed to Sangay large enough
for several families to share. Over the door was
mounted a demon-trap of crossed sticks and
coloured thread.

Inside, it could have been any house in
Sangay's own village: windowless and dark, the
air thick with smoke, the walls and roof-beams
blackened by generations of caked soot. Pots
steamed and bubbled on the hearth. He could
smell incense, dung-smoke, drying skins. A but-
ter-lamp flickered before the household
shrine. There were people everywhere — old
women dozing by the fire, children tumbling
in corners, neighbours with muddy feet and
rain-soaked garments wandering in and out. So
much did it put him in mind of his own home
that he felt his throat tighten and his eyes sting.
In that dark crowded room no one could see
or hear his grief; tears ran down his cheeks and
he did not bother to wipe them away.

Then one of the women poured butter-tea
into his bowl, and Wanjur called him to the
hearthside to share in a meal of stew and

buckwheat cakes, washed down by *chang*. Finally the meal ended, and leaf-wrapped betel nuts were ceremoniously handed round. Drowsy with food and drink, the fire's warmth, and his long day's journey, Sangay let his chin droop upon his chest. But it seemed there was to be little sleep for him that night. Earlier in the day a wandering storyteller, a *manip*, had arrived in the village with his tales of Lord Buddha and the holy saints; and of Guru Rimpoche the Lotus-Born, bringer of the true wisdom to Druk-yul. The *manip* must have been as weary as Sangay, for he had been performing all afternoon outside the temple. Now half the folk of the village had crowded into the headman's house, demanding one last story before they slept.

Once again the *manip* opened his wooden cabinet with its many small compartments, each one showing a scene from some tale of marvels. To Sangay's disappointment it was too dark inside the hut to see the pictures; but when the story began, he forgot this and all other sorrows.

"Now listen," said the *manip*, "to the tale of Pema Lingpa the Treasure-Seeker, he who was called Son of the Lotus Grove, the greatest of all dance-makers and the true incarnation of Guru Rimpoche.

"In his youth he was a blacksmith, a maker of swords and coats of mail for the mightiest warriors of Druk-yul; and of temple-bells whose tone was of surpassing beauty. He was a small man, some say of dwarf-like stature, but like all smiths he was vigorous and strong.

"One day Pema Lingpa went out into the forest in search of mushrooms, a dish of which he was exceptionally fond. On the forest path he met an ancient hermit with the long beard and five-sided hat of a *naljorpa*. Pema Lingpa would have liked to offer the hermit some mushrooms as a token of his respect, but alas, he had not found a single one. When he explained this to the hermit, the old man told him to dig among the twigs and leaf-mould beneath a certain pine tree."

The *manip* paused; there was a breathless silence. They all knew what Pema Lingpa had found beneath the pine tree, yet each time heard it from the storyteller's lips with the same thrill of surprise.

"There," said the *manip*, "was a whole bed of the largest and most succulent mushrooms that Pema Lingpa had ever seen!

" 'Indeed,' said Pema Lingpa, 'you are a clever old man, as well as a holy one. You must come with me to my hut. I will cook these mushrooms in butter, and you will share them with me.'

"As they set out together for Pema Lingpa's hut, the hermit pressed something into Pema Lingpa's hand; it was a scrap of paper, tightly rolled.

" 'Do not look at it yet,' said the old man. 'Put it away in the pocket of your *kho*.' And Pema Lingpa did as he was bid.

"When they reached Pema Lingpa's hut, the blacksmith stoked up the fire and cooked the mushrooms with five kinds of savoury herbs. But when he looked around for the hermit to tell him the meal was ready, the old man had vanished. Pema Lingpa searched everywhere, wandering among the trees that grew beside his hut and calling out again and again in a great voice, but there was no reply. And so he ate the mushrooms himself.

"That night, just as he was on the edge of sleep, Pema Lingpa remembered the paper that the hermit had given him. There, he thought, might be the explanation of the old man's strange behavior. Pema Lingpa unrolled the paper, but of course, being only a simple blacksmith and not a monk, he could not read a single word of what was written there."

At these words there was a small stirring among the crowd, a hum of disappointment.

"In any case," the *manip* went on, "the message was written in the old script, the Cloud-spirit Writing handed down by the gods themselves, which none save a few scholar-monks of the Old Sect, the *Nyingmapa*, could understand."

In the firelit dark, his listeners nodded sagely. Clearly they had heard of this ancient writing.

"At that moment," said the storyteller, "a mysterious voice seemed to speak in Pema Lingpa's ear, reading aloud the message on the paper."

" 'Go to the Burning Lake,' the voice said. 'There you will find hidden treasure.'

"Pema Lingpa rushed to the door of his hut and looked out.

" 'Who speaks to me?' he cried in bewilderment."

The *manip's* listeners howled with delight; they knew the answer.

"On the first night of the full moon that followed, Pema Lingpa and his uncle, who was a lay-monk, and his uncle's wife, journeyed to a lake hidden in the high forest. It was called the Burning Lake because of the strange lights that danced and flickered on the surface of its waters. It was thought to be inhabited by snake gods, and the people of that region were afraid to approach it. But the fearless blacksmith and his uncle walked to the very edge of the moonlit shore.

"Just as Pema Lingpa was wondering how he should begin to look for the treasure, he heard a great wind roaring around his ears, and he felt himself dragged down and down into the dark waters of the lake. Soon he was standing before a temple, marvellously decorated, with endless numbers of doors; but only one door stood open. Guarding it was a hideous old woman with one eye and one long tooth like a tiger's fang.

" 'Stand aside, good mother,' said Pema Lingpa. 'I have work here that I must finish, and so I must go through that door.'

" 'No one goes through that door,' the old woman replied, and her voice was like the shrill and bitter sound of the winter wind. Her one eye seemed like a dead grey stone in her wrinkled face.

"Though she appeared to have no more weight or substance than a withered leaf, Pema Lingpa did not wish to push her aside. He had been taught to respect those older than himself, and besides, the sound of her voice and the look in her dreadful eye struck cold fear into his heart.

"At a loss as to know what he should do, Pema Lingpa stood shivering in the depths of the Burning Lake. He could see through the windows of the temple the yellow glimmer of altar-lamps, but he could not enter. Then he remembered the scroll that the hermit had given him. He drew it out of the breast of his *kho* where he had hidden it, and held it up for the old woman to see.

"Carefully she read the message that was written there, and though she made no move to stand aside, Pema Lingpa now saw that she was holding a jewelled casket in her hands.

" 'The Precious Guru has left this for you,' she said, and suddenly her voice had changed, had become as sweet and soft as the winds of spring.

"Pema Lingpa took the casket. Before he could thank the old woman, she had stepped through the open door and had shut it after her.

"Now Pema Lingpa wondered how to reach the surface of the lake, burdened as he was with the jewelled casket, which seemed as heavy as though it were filled with lead. But soon the whistling, wailing sound of the wind returned, and a strong current swept him up and up until his head broke through the dark waters and he smelled the cold mountain air.

"He waded to shore, and showed the casket to his uncle and to his old aunt who, gathering up her courage, had come down to the verge to see what was happening.

"His aunt shrieked and tore her hair when she saw the casket. 'Alas,' she cried, 'you foolish one, you have stolen this treasure from the snake gods who dwell beneath the lake, and now they will come after us and kill us.'

"But his uncle the lay-monk smiled, for he knew of the hermit who had visited Pema Lingpa's hut, and the strange voice that had spoken in Pema Lingpa's head.

" 'We are indeed blessed,' his uncle said, 'for that old man of the forest must have been Guru Rimpoche himself, and he has shown you where to find his treasure as a sign that you, Pema Lingpa, are his true incarnation, his embodiment on this earth.'

"Pema Lingpa's uncle and aunt hurried home to tell everyone this wonderful news, and to organize a celebration in the village. But Pema Lingpa shut himself in the smallest temple and refused to come out. He was confused and afraid, for he was a simple man with no knowledge of religion, who could neither read nor write; who had never been taught and had no idea how to teach others. But night after night he sat by the altar, praying to Guru Rimpoche for guidance. Then one night he looked up to see a whole band of Cloud-spirits dancing in the light of the butter-lamps. 'Go to sleep,' they told him. 'In the morning all things will be made clear.'

"And so Pema Lingpa slept, with the jewelled casket in his arms; and in his sleep the Cloud-spirits filled his mind with knowledge, like a great light burning behind his eyes.

"When he woke, he saw the casket lying open before him. It was filled with scripts covered with the ancient writing of the gods, which was as clear to him now as though the Guru himself were reading the words aloud.

"That morning Pema Lingpa went forth and began to teach the villages what he had learned, and while he spoke, thousands of blossoms, in all colours of the rainbow, fell down out of the sky, vanishing like snowflakes as they touched the earth."

There may have been more to the story, but Sangay, in spite of himself, had fallen sound asleep. Once again strange dreams visited him, but on this night they were happy dreams, of bands of Cloud-spirits, and a moon-drenched lake, and secret treasure, and flowers tumbling like coloured snowflakes out of a summer sky.

When he woke in the grey half-light of dawn, his mind was filled with beautiful visions, and

he imagined how it would be when he reached
the White Leopard Dzong. Surely the Precious
Guru would visit him, as he had visited Pema
Lingpa. All the monks, from the Abbot and the
Superior Monks to the postulants like himself,
would acknowledge Sangay as the true incarnation of the Guru. And his mother and father,
and his brother Norbu, and the baby Llamo,
and perhaps even his cousin Dechen would
come to the festival held in his honour. He
would be showered with gifts, and he too would
become a Treasure Seeker. . . . Sangay drifted
back to sleep until Wanjur, saying "Up, up, lazy
one!" unrolled him from his rug like a badly
wrapped package and spilled him onto the
hard-packed floor.

Temples and Towers

The massive inward-sloping walls of the White Leopard Dzong clung to the rocky heights above a river-gorge. Its many roofs of silvered shingles glimmered in the early sunlight. From west to east, from north to south, it commanded all the roads that crossed the valley.

Sangay stood beside Wanjur on the stony river-bank, staring up at the Dzong. Hanging there on the sheer brink of the ravine, its walls white as ice below their broad band of holy scarlet, its roofs forested with prayer-flags, it seemed to Sangay like a dwelling-place of gods.

It was the third day of their journey. Half-fearful, half-impatient, he asked Wanjur, "Will we be there by dark?"

"By midday, if you pick up your feet," said Wanjur, leaping nimbly across a rock-fall. Sangay loosened his sandal, dug another pebble from under his heel, and trudged after Wanjur.

It was not yet midday when they climbed the steep road to the gates of the fortress-monastery. They stopped once to catch their breath and once to put on the *kabney* — the wide white scarf worn as a mark of respect when entering the Dzong. Fumbling with this swathe of fabric three times as long as himself, Sangay managed to trail both ends through the dirt. Patiently Wanjur helped him to drape the *kabney* across his chest and twice over his shoulder in the customary way.

They reached the top of a broad flight of stone steps. The older monks were breathing hard. The Chief Monk used an end of his sash to wipe sweat out of his eyes. Sangay's own heart was banging against his ribs — though more from sheer fright than from the effort of the climb. He took a long, slow breath as the senior monk thumped the dragon-headed knocker, and the high bronze-banded gates swung open.

Within was a stone-paved courtyard and, on either side, long balconies resting on intricately carved red-painted posts. In the middle of the courtyard rose the tall central tower, the *utse*, with its shining white walls, its carved and painted windows and glittering golden pinnacles.

Everywhere there were monks, bare-footed, russet-robed, turning prayer-wheels or going quietly about their chores. Old men half-dozed in the sunlight, making a gentle bee-hum as they endlessly droned their mantras. A shaven-headed novice, not much older than Sangay, pounded tea in a wooden churn. Small red-robed boys peered out of doorways and trundled, self-important, intent on mysterious errands, along the pillared galleries. Cats drowsed on doorsills; cockerels roosted in corners; a large shaggy dog slept head on paws beside the tower.

Sangay's six companions had already set down their packs and were sitting lotus-fashion, comfortably at rest, on the sun-warmed stones. In a moment or two a smiling novice brought them rice and butter-tea. Sangay was ravenous; he had not eaten since the hour before dawn.

He held out his cup and, hot though the tea was, drained it to the dregs. He had barely time to finish his rice when a monk began to beat on a gong from one of the high balconies of the *utse*, summoning everyone inside to prayer.

Sangay followed Wanjur through the tower doors of beaten copper. At once he was lost in a maze of stairwells, ladders, twisting passageways.

They climbed, and climbed again, ascending skyward through these innermost secret pathways of the Dzong. Sangay thought, as he climbed, of the concentric circles of heaven: the oceans, golden mountains and vast continents surrounding the sacred mountain of Meru. He knew little of religion — only what his uncle the village lay-priest had told him, on long winter evenings by the fire. But that much he remembered — the circles endlessly enclosing circles, like an onion's layers, until one came at last to Og-min, the final heaven at the far reaches of the universe, beyond which lay perpetual dark.

At every level of the tower there were temple-rooms, each one more wonderful than the last. There were rooms of ivory, silver and peacock feathers; rooms where turquoise and gold embroidered dragons danced on canopies of crimson silk; rooms filled with silken banners; rooms in which the floors were paved with silver, amber and lapis lazuli. And from every wall, from every niche and alcove, the gods looked down.

There were many-headed gods with a thousand eyes and arms; wrathful gods with hideous, livid faces, armed with scorpions, scimitars and thunderbolts; gods with the heads of serpents, snow-bears, yaks and vultures, bearing skull-bowls, thigh-bone trumpets, dragon-drums. So terrible were these images, so like the creatures of his darkest dreams, that Sangay shrank back against the wall and covered his face with his two hands.

He felt Wanjur's hand fall gently on his shoulder. "Be not afraid, Sangay. These are only the apparitions the soul sees after death. They are illusions only — the inventions of our own minds."

As well, there were images of gentler gods. Here was the Lotus Lord of Dance, surrounded by clouds of fairy-beings. Here too were the Kings of the Four Directions, wrapped in swirling smoke and flame; mighty Guru Rimpoche on his flying tiger; and White Tara, the Lady of the Mountains. And everywhere one looked, one saw Lord Buddha — hundreds upon hundreds of golden Buddha-figures, glimmering in the light of a thousand butter-lamps.

On they went, climbing and climbing through the many-levelled tower, through endless-seeming tiers of temples. Sangay's head throbbed. His eyes were dazzled.

High up in the *utse* they came to a room where fifty or more monks sat in long rows with strips of parchment spread out in front of them. They were not so much chanting as shouting, as though each monk was determined to drown all the others out, and each one seemed to be shouting a different set of words.

"What are they doing?" asked Sangay, raising his own voice over the din as he stood with Wanjur in the open doorway.

"They are reading from the sacred scriptures. It is a very important ritual. They must go on without stopping until they have read every word."

"How long will that take?" asked Sangay, curious.

"Many weeks," said Wanjur. "One day you, too, will sit in this room, and read from the sacred writings."

For *weeks*? thought Sangay, trying to imagine it. He glanced up to see if Wanjur was joking, but the young monk's face was solemn.

They climbed another ladder, and now Sangay could hear music — gongs, flutes, bells, cymbals. The sound ceased suddenly, and was replaced by the soft ebb and flow of chanting.

At last they had reached the highest temple, at the dizzying summit of the tower, stepping into a warm sweet-scented darkness that shimmered with the yellow light of altar lamps. Again Sangay saw the golden glint of the Buddha's image, repeated a thousand-fold.

Rows of monks faced one another along the central aisle, holding dragon-painted scarlet drums, trumpets of ebony and silver, bells, cymbals, conch shells.

Another monk sat before an altar heaped with bread and fruit and rice, in a luminous fog of incense smoke. With one hand he held a small brass bell, in the other the sacred thunderbolt of Druk-yul.

The mantra rose and swelled and faded like the wind; the gentle music played. The monk at the altar rang his bell and twirled his sacred thunderbolt. Sangay sat still as stone, for fear of breaking the spell. He would never be able to tell Dechen about these things.

***

Sangay spent that first night in the Dzong in a room with five other boys, all younger than himself; when the gong sounded for morning prayers, he was sure that he had not slept at all. Shivering in the raw grey air, he followed his fellow postulants into the chanting-hall. He was bewildered, frightened; his eyes felt as though there was sand behind the lids. Yet in spite of it all, his heart raced with excitement. Yesterday, in the temple-tower, he had glimpsed a world of wonders; now, in this vast, cold, half-lit hall, what further marvels might await?

At the front of the room were three huge images of the Buddha, each one twice the height of a tall man. They were covered from head to foot in gold plate, and in the forehead of each was a Third Eye of blue-green stone.

Gods and demons looked down from the frescoes on the walls, and from the painted scrolls that hung from every gallery and pillar.

Sangay could see, on a high dais, what must surely be the Abbot's throne, though today the Abbot was not in it. There were, as well, three smaller thrones. One was occupied by the monk who conducted the music and led the chanting, one by the monk who seemed to be in charge of time-tables. On the third sat a stern-faced official with a whip in one hand and a rod in the other.

"Is that the *chostimpa*?" whispered Sangay, nudging the boy who sat next to him. He had already heard stories of this pitiless monk who kept order in the prayer-hall. He possessed a hundred hidden eyes, the novices said; eyes which missed no smallest infraction of the rules.

"Yes," the other boy hissed back, behind his hand. "Now be quiet, before he sees you. We are not permitted to speak in the chanting-hall."

Distantly, across that cavernous room, Sangay caught a glimpse of Wanjur, looking sober and pious as he stared towards the wall with inward-gazing eyes. When the morning tea and rice were brought in, Sangay looked around for his friend, but could see no sign of him. Excitement was giving way to fatigue and a sudden fierce and unexpected loneliness. His throat ached, and the raw cold of the prayer-hall was creeping into his bones. He stirred his puffed rice into his butter-tea, and swallowed it without much appetite.

Tending the yaks all day on the high pasture, he had escaped from loneliness and boredom by making up dances in his head. But that old habit of mind would not serve him now. There was too much in this place that was new and strange, too much that he did not understand, too much that he was expected to remember. He could find no pattern in it.

The chanting began again. Bells rang, gyalings wailed, the deep-voiced trumpets rumbled. Sangay crouched at the back of the hall near the door, afraid to move, afraid almost to breathe. His cramped legs were starting to hurt, yet he dared not shift position. Not for an instant could he forget the presence of the *chostimpa* scowling down from his high seat,

with his rod and his terrible knotted whip at
hand.

After what seemed an eternity, there was
another interval between prayers. Hot tea arrived in wooden buckets, and as Sangay tilted
his cup to drain the dregs, he looked over the
rim into Wanjur's cheerful gaze.

"And did you sleep well last night?" Wanjur
inquired.

"No," replied Sangay, and reminded of how
weary he was, he yawned.

Wanjur laughed. "No more did I, my first
night in the Dzong. It will be different tonight.
There are few enough hours for sleep, and you
will soon learn not to waste them. I came to give
you a message, Sangay. You are to go to the
cloister of the Superior Monk Rigdzin Godem,
who has agreed to accept you as his acolyte."

Sangay looked up in dismay. "But I thought
I would be *your* acolyte."

"Not mine, my small friend," Wanjur said.
"I am only a dancer. I cannot teach you the
things a novice must learn — to write, to read
the scriptures, to recite the litany. Rigdzin
Godem is not known as an easy taskmaster, but
he is a good man, just and fair. From him you

will learn quickly, and learn well. But now I must go, for listen, the prayers are beginning again."

***

"How old are you?" asked Rigdzin Godem. Sangay gazed up in terror at the tall monk with the searching eyes and stern unsmiling mouth. Rigdzin Godem's robes were spotlessly clean, falling in precise, unrumpled folds. They smelled of lamp-oil and sandalwood.

"Well?" prompted Rigdzin Godem. Sangay's tongue froze in his head.

"Eight, Master," he finally managed to say in a strangled whisper.

Rigdzin Godem made a noise in his throat, which could have meant anything. "Old to begin," he remarked. "Well, at first you will be taking your lessons with boys half your age and a third your size. But no matter. You look intelligent. If you are diligent you can make up for lost time." He said this absently, as though it signified little to him, one way or another. "You may sleep here," he said, indicating a corner of his large, cold, sparsely furnished cell. "Tomorrow we will make a beginning."

***

For Sangay, the days became an an unvarying succession of hours endlessly repeated, like a mantra. Those days began long before the sun rose over the eastern peaks, and ended as they had begun, by the glow of butter-lamps. He learned to sit motionless for hours in the lotus position, ankles resting on tops of thighs. In the mornings he memorized creed, incantation, liturgy — those words in which each sound, each letter was in itself sacred, a spell waiting to be released by the power of joined voices. After morning devotions came a frugal breakfast, then interminable reading lessons. Sangay pored over the long pale leaves of parchment inscribed with elegant, enigmatic black figures. Little by little they yielded up their mysterious messages, as his knowledge and his understanding grew.

There was a meal — usually red rice and stewed vegetables — at midday. The monks did not (as Dechen had gloomily predicted) exist on nothing but rice and tea. They had soup with meat and sometimes dumplings, curd and wheat-cakes in the afternoon, and soup again at night. The monastery was by no means a poor one, and it was well-managed; there was always enough to eat. Late in the day there was more reading of scriptures; in the evenings, as the shadows closed in, there was chanting, and after the lamps were lit, more lessons still. What he was to remember of those first days was perpetual fatigue, the chill dampness of stone under his bare feet — and a never-ceasing hum in the air, like the buzz of insects. And there was always music — music felt, after a time, instead of heard, like the sounds his own body made when he stopped his ears: the heart-thud of drums, wind-sigh of conch-shells, tap of timbrels, soft moan of clarionets.

He became a *gaylong* — a novice. His head was shaved and he put on the russet robes of monkhood. He memorized endless holy texts, he learned to perform a myriad of minor rites and, after a fashion, to play the sacred instruments. He studied the life of the Buddha, and the life of Guru Rimpoche. He memorized the Four Noble Truths and the Steps of the Eight-Fold Path. Each day he practised, as well as he could, the laws of faith, honesty, patience, meekness, gentleness, forbearance.

Swaying rhythmically to and fro, he repeated the syllables of power. Though he did not always understand the words, he felt the magic in them.

Once a pilgrim travelling through their village had sheltered for the night with Sangay's family. He had paid for his meal and his place by the fire by telling them of the great walled city to the east that he had once visited. The Dzong was like that imagined city — a place of bewildering complexity, with spaces meant for many purposes: kitchens, storerooms, armory, assembly hall, school, library, temples, hospitals, hostels and private dwellings, linked by courtyards, staircases, passageways. And beyond the golden-pinnacled tower at the centre of the Dzong were doorways leading into the still more mysterious world where the Dzongda, the Lord of the Dzong, and his officials had their offices.

***

Sangay's arrow, too hastily released, landed halfway down the field. "A feeble effort," said the archery-master Jigme Llendrup, and the *gaylongs* settled down to a familiar lecture.

"Remember, there are monks in this very monastery," said Jigme Llendrup, "who fought against the armies of Khang-yul. And we are no more than a generation away from the last great civil war. You may think that here in the monastery you may hide from the troubles of the world, yet every monk must be ready if need be to defend the Dzong."

He stepped behind Sangay, reaching round to correct his grip. "Now try again," he said. But it took a strong and skilful bowman to send an arrow the full length of the field, to strike a target a hundred and thirty metres distant. The young monks shot for exercise and for amusement. None of them expected to hit the target, and would have been astonished if they had. Even at a tournament of experienced marksmen, the target might be struck only a few times in the course of the day.

Still, every day that he had time to spare from prayers and study, Sangay would take his practice-bow to the archery-grounds. He liked to imagine he was a famous warrior-monk like the ones in the Dance of Heroes: his head crowned with the Rings of Knighthood, a sword-belt girdling his pleated robe, a rhinoceros-skin buckler on his arm. He yearned with all his heart for a great sword like the one the Dzongda wore.

***

The days sped by, punctuated with the sound of gongs and trumpets, calling him to duties, to prayers, to meals, to sleep. And in his nostrils always was the monastery smell — the rank odour of burning dung, the reek of butter-lamps, mixed with a pungent incense sweetness.

He was obedient in all things, and quick to learn, and did not too often feel the smart of his teacher's rod. If he was unhappy, he had little time to realize it. He was, as Wanjur had said, too busy to grieve. When he thought of his family, or of Dechen, he found that their faces were fading from his memory, like faces in a dream. Only in the brief instant before he fell asleep on his narrow mat in Rigdzin Godem's cell, or in that twilight space between sleeping and waking, did he sometimes feel a pang of longing for the high pastures, the wind and sun and the wide blue air.

THE DANCE OF GODS
AND DEMONS

Midwinter approached, bringing with it the great events of the turning year. Domchoe, the Excellent Ritual, had come and gone. Demons had been appeased, the favor of the gods invoked. Now the monastery was preparing to celebrate Tsechhu, the Tenth Day Festival. All day long, to the booming of horns and the rhythmic clash of cymbals, the senior monks sculpted butter-images, performed the New Year's rituals, and rehearsed the sacred dances. For the novices, there were other, less interesting tasks.

"When they chose you to be a monk," said Sangay to Yenten Tshering, "did you know you would be spending so much time cleaning *tashigomangs?*" He picked up his rag and started to polish yet another of the small, ornately decorated shrines. His fingers were stiff with cold. With Tsechhu approaching there were no spare moments to huddle over the kitchen fire. From dawn until long after the lamps were lit the novices swept and cleaned and polished, scrubbed pots, ground chili-peppers, pounded tea.

"It keeps us humble, my tutor says." Yenten Tshering sat back on his heels. He had finished his *tashigomang*. He was a small, serious-minded boy, dutiful and uncomplaining. "My family are coming to the festival," he told Sangay. "Are yours?"

"Your family lives in the next valley." When Yenten Tshering gave him a reproachful look, Sangay realized how sharply he had spoken. Other families came to the Dzong at festival time to visit their sons. But his village was so far away, over so many mountains, across so many valleys . . .

He rubbed harder, and thought instead about the time, still four years hence, when he would be old enough to learn the sacred dances.

"When you are thirteen I will ask the dance-master to consider it," Rigdzin Godem had told him. "Not a moment sooner. You are quick with your mind, there's no denying that. It will not take long for you to grasp the principles. But to put them into practice, for the body to work perfectly in accord with the mind — I have seen you tripping over the hem of your robe, Sangay, and bumping your head against a beam because your thoughts were else-where . . . No, it will take some growing up, and maybe a magic spell or two, to make a dancer of you."

Sangay had to be content with that. But he was drawn to the practice-hall as a fly to the butter vat; and one day close to the time of Tsechhu, when he knew that the monks would be rehearsing in costume, he offered a handful of hoarded biscuits and his broom to fat, lazy Phuntsho Zangpo, who had been assigned to fill the butter-lamps.

"Sweep this floor for me," Sangay said, "and I will tend to the lamps in the practice-hall." He left Phuntsho with a mouthful of biscuit, making half-hearted passes at the flag-stones, and set off to watch the dancers.

Luck was with him: today the monks were practising the Drum Dance of Dramitse. Of all the tales he had heard since coming to the Dzong, the story of the Drum Dance was his favourite. Once, long ago, the learned lama Kunga Gyaltshen, descendant of the great dance-maker Pema Lingpa, had traveled in a vision to Zangdog-pelri, the Copper-Clad Mountain. There, in the celestial palace of Guru Rimpoche, he had witnessed a wonderful dance in which the Guru's attendants were transformed into a hundred peaceful and terrifying gods. When Kunga Gyaltshen returned to the human world he taught this dance to his disciples, and now it was performed throughout the land of Druk-yul.

Sangay stood in a shadowy corner of the hall, the lamps forgotten. All the dancers wore the masks of animal-headed gods — serpent, snow-lion, eagle, hound — yet he knew at a glance which one was Wanjur. There was no mistaking the sureness of Wanjur's step, his lithe grace, as he performed the first slow, dreamlike movements of the ancient dance.

All the dancers carried drums, which they beat with thin curved sticks. Their costumes of rose and amber silks were skirted with a mass of swirling, floating scarves.

Now the slow, stately rhythm of the dance changed, gathering speed and energy as it built to its leaping, whirling climax. The drums, echoing every step, made a noise like thunder. As the last notes died away and the dancers prepared to leave the floor, Sangay still watched wide-eyed from his corner, while all around him the butter-lamps sputtered and winked out. Presently Wanjur appeared at his side, maskless, unwinding the long strip of cloth that protected the lower part of his face. No longer was he a leaping, bounding lion-headed demon, but a round-faced, smiling young man with sweat dripping into his eyes.

"That," said Sangay on a long breath, "was the most wonderful dance I have ever seen."

"Was it?" Wanjur was panting a little. He wiped his forearm across his face. "Well, soon enough you will have a part in it."

"Not soon," said Sangay mournfully. "Rigdzin Godem says I must wait four more years."

"They will pass in the blink of an eye," said Wanjur. "And believe me, my young friend, when you have spent your first day on the practice-floor, when every muscle in your body cries out and your legs are black and blue from the dance-master's stick, then you will pray to the gods to turn back the wheel and make you nine again."

***

"My body is like a mountain," Rigdzin Godem intoned. "Reflect on this."

It was the hour of midday meditation. Sangay breathed in, breathed out, let his body relax, his mind empty of thought. He was the mountain, rising from the earth, and he was a part of that earth. He was the mountain battered by storms, as his body was battered by the ceaseless demands of daily life.

"My eyes are like deep mountain lakes," said Rigdzin Godem. "Meditate on this."

Everything I see, thought Sangay, is but a cloud-shadow moving upon the water.

"My mind is like the sky," Rigdzin Godem said. And Sangay saw his thoughts dissolving like summer clouds in the void of heaven.

Mountains. Cloud shadows. The blue roof of the sky. A flood of memories rushed in to fill the empty vessel of his mind. "No one achieves true selflessness," Rigdzin Godem liked to tell the young monks, "when he clings to thoughts of home and family. These too are illusion. Cut yourself free from them."

But could he ever cut himself free from his memories? Once again he was in a place where the air smelled of juniper and summer grasses and the only music was the sighing of the wind. He thought of how he used to make dances in his head, when hours went by too slowly. Prayer-flags and sun and wind and clouds, all spinning and turning together in a pattern of his own imagining . . .

"Sangay Tenzing!" Rigdzin Godem's voice jolted him back to the world as harshly as a rod across the shoulders. He looked up, blinking. "Yes, Master?"

Rigdzin Godem's mouth was set in a thin, hard line. "Were you so deep in meditation," he asked, "that you did not hear my voice?"

"Yes, Master," said Sangay.

"That is an untruth," said his tutor, flatly. "Three times I spoke to you, Sangay Tenzing, and you did not hear. Clearly, you were in another world. Meditation is a remedy against disturbing emotions. It is a release from thought. It is not an escape from obligation — nor is it a means of idle entertainment. You disappoint me, Sangay Tenzing. If you behave in this way, you will continue to disappoint me. Now go."

***

Sangay gave the postulant Dawa Khandro a sharp elbow in the ribs and pushed to the front of the balcony. Now he could see the royal cavalcade approaching up the steep road to the Dzong — four hundred men and four hundred horses, one of the *gaylongs* whispered, awestruck. Welcome fires had been lit all along the steep approach. For weeks the monks had spoken of little else. For the first time in a generation the Druk Desi, king of the land of Druk-yul, had chosen to celebrate the Winter Festival at the White Leopard Dzong. It was a great honour — and a sign, Rigdzin Godem declared, of the great esteem in which their monastery was held.

Now, after the long weeks of waiting, and whispering, and imagining, there beneath

their very walls was the royal court of Druk-yul
— nobles, musicians, archers, warriors, servants, priests — a river of bright colour shifting
and swirling under the ice-white walls of the
Dzong. Banners and pennants rippled in the
wind; silk umbrellas nodded and swayed like
gaudy flowers; above, on the high balconies,
gyalings, flutes and tabors made a festive music.
And there in the midst of all that wondrous
confusion, resplendent in saffron scarf and
scarlet cloak, was the Druk Desi himself. Sangay
clung with both hands to the balustrade. This
was a sight he might not see again in several
lifetimes, and he did not intend to miss it.

As the royal entourage reached the fortress
stairs, a band of guest-dancers from the nearby
village swarmed out of the gates and down the
steps. Leaping and stamping, bright skirts
swinging, headdresses flapping, they cleared
the way with thunderbolt steps — trampling
underfoot any stray demons who might bar the
path. And here was the Dzongda, striding down
the steps to greet his monarch in snow-white
shirt and crimson *kho*, with the long red scarf
of his office thrown over his shoulder, and his
ceremonial sword at his side. Up the broad

steps strewn with yellow winter-blooming flowers, through the great gates and across the
courtyards of the Dzong marched the royal
procession. In honour of the occasion the
monks had hung a wonderful *thanka* out over
the wall of the temple-court. With golden
thread on joined pieces of silk, it depicted Guru
Rimpoche astride the tiger's back. It was the
greatest treasure of the monastery; Rigdzin
Godem had said that anyone of pure heart who
saw it, and prayed before it, would be sure to
attain enlightenment.

The air was filled with chanting, and the
sweet cleansing smoke of fragrant branches.
The long brass trumpets bellowed and
snarled; the fifes and tabors sounded. And so
the king came to the White Leopard Dzong,
while Sangay stared, and marvelled, and forgot all the tasks that had been assigned to
him.

In four years, Sangay promised himself with
fierce resolve, in four years I will learn the
Drum Dance of Dramitse. And one day I will
dance it before the King.

***

Every day in the temple-court there was singing, dancing, music-making. The Tenth Day Festival was as much a public entertainment as a sacred New Year's ritual. People from all the surrounding valleys crowded into the Dzong to meet and gossip with their neighbours, to take part in the archery competition, and to watch the sacred dancing. The village folk drank a great deal of chang, and feasted on rice and chilis from their bamboo picnic baskets. The *atsaras* in their big-nosed comic masks and baggy trousers mingled with the dancers, cheerfully mimicking their steps. No one, not even a king's courtier, was safe from the *atsaras*' mockery. The onlookers howled with laughter at their antics and their rude, irreverent jokes.

The celebrations finished, on New Year's Day, with the Festival of Losar and the Dance of Gods and Demons. This day — the one on which Lord Buddha and his servant Guru Rimpoche had vanquished the demon-forces from the land of Druk-yul — was the most auspicious of the year.

Sangay woke that New Year's dawn to a thunderous bellowing of trumpets. The Dance had begun; it would go on till nightfall. He threw on his robe, and ran to join the jostling, excited crowd that filled the temple-court. Soon the chanting began, and a soft wailing music that was like the sound of the wind in the high hill-passes. The death-spirits led off the dance, bounding and cavorting in their red and white skull-masks. Then the sorcerer-priests appeared in their towering black-fringed hats, dancing to a slow, sombre music. They were dressed in wide-sleeved robes of silk brocade, in brilliant shades of emerald, gold and scarlet, their aprons decorated with thunderbolts and hideous, scowling faces. After them came the demons, throng upon throng of animal-headed beings from the invisible realms, leaping and capering with wild abandon. Solemn though the dance was, Sangay felt a great urge to laugh. Indeed, he could see that the onlookers — villagers, tribespeople, even the king's courtiers — were holding their sides with merriment. He reminded himself that for those who were not monks, who did not understand the hidden Mystery of the dance, it was a mere spectacle, an entertainment.

In the centre of the temple-court lay the *dorma*, the sacrificial figure made of clay, surrounded by the magic triangle of power. Again and again the demons leaped, bounded, whirled around the triangle, until the sorcerers subdued them one by one with mystic gestures and drove them into the clay body of the *dorma*. The demon-dance went on for hours, while trumpets wailed and howled, drums thudded, cymbals crashed. On and on they danced, the demons in their grotesque masks, the sorcerers in their silken robes and tall black hats; at times with quick, spinning, whirling steps, hats nodding, scarves twirling; at other times as slowly as dancers in a dream.

"Will this thing never end?" complained Phuntsho Zangpo, edging next to Sangay. "I am faint with hunger." But Sangay had forgotten his cold feet and growling stomach. He was using all the mind-skills the monks had taught him to burn into his memory the intricate patterns of the dance.

And now the powers of good were gaining victory, as group after group of demons appeared and were exorcised by the sorcerers. At last there appeared the splendid figure of Guru

Rimpoche himself, and all the demons, bowing down before him, vanished. Then came the chant of final exorcism:

Hum! Through the blessing of the blood-drinking Fierce One, may the injuring demons and evil spirits be kept at bay. I pierce their hearts with this hook; I bind their hands with this snare of rope; I bind their bodies with this powerful chain; I keep them down with the tinkling bell.

The sun hung low in the sky. The long shadows of the wizards' hats lay in strange shapes across the courtyard. And then the horned god of the underworld, the Bull-Headed Lord of Death, appeared, and with the three-edged sacred dagger stabbed the *dorma* through and through. It was Wanjur, this year, who danced the part of this fierce and vengeful deity. At once graceful and ferocious, he moved with terrible composure through the measured cadences, the intricate, elaborate steps. Wanjur danced, thought Sangay, watching spellbound, as though he was possessed by the god himself.

The dance ended with the ritual burning of the *dorma*.

Almost at the instant that the tinder caught and the sacred fire flared up, a light snow, like a message from the gods, began to fall. "Snow at Losar," whispered the monks upon the balconies; and in the temple-court the villagers sent up a great shout of joy. They could have prayed for no more auspicious sign. The old year, with its demons of ill-luck, was dead; the new year, filled with promise, had begun.

THE BAMBOO BOW

Four years went by, like the turning of a prayer wheel. Sangay grew taller; his voice, intoning the mantras, cracked, then deepened.

In his thirteenth summer, anxious and awkward and only half in control of his rapidly lengthening limbs, he was summoned before the dance-master, Penjor Karpo.

"Stand up straight," said Penjor Karpo. "Pull your shoulders back. Let me see you walk across the practice-floor."

Loose-jointed, heavy-footed, sick with nervousness, Sangay ambled to the far side of the room. He was painfully aware of the dance-master's scrutiny.

"Again," said Penjor Karpo severely. This time things might have gone better, had not

Sangay stumbled and half-fallen over a mat left
lying beside the door.

"Now come here," said Penjor Karpo, sighing. He considered Sangay's hands, hanging
graceless as plucked birds at the ends of his
narrow wrists. Frowning, he pondered the gan-
gling, loose-limbed frame, the large, bare, un-
washed feet.

"How old did you say you were?"

"Thirteen, Master."

"Past time, I suppose," said Penjor Karpo.
"Well, I must think further on this. Come back
after the Day of Blessed Rain." And Sangay left
the dance-floor in bitter disappointment, all his
eager expectations crushed.

Autumn came, and the Rain Festival. Sangay
returned to the practice-floor, and once again
Penjor Karpo thought hard, and shook his
head. Two more months went by. Rigdzin
Godem sent a polite reminder to the dance-
master that in the spring his pupil Sangay would
be fourteen. Only then did Penjor Karpo con-
cede that Sangay's dance lessons could no
longer be postponed.

In his own youth Penjor Karpo had been a
dancer of legendary skill; now he was known for

his knife-edged tongue and his lack of patience. Other lessons — reading, writing, liturgy — came easily to Sangay: the dance did not. Though there were twenty novices in the class, it seemed that the full weight of Penjor Karpo's temper fell on Sangay.

They began with the hand-drum: an exhausting business, for the small drum had to be held in the right hand with the arm at full stretch for an hour at a time. The trick was to turn the wrist quickly so that a pair of weights suspended from cords rapped against the vellum. Meanwhile the left hand rang a small brass bell. Hour after hour they practised, till Sangay's arm felt like a stick of wood attached to his aching shoulder. For a long time he could not manage it all.

Thwack, went the dance-master's rod across Sangay's shins, when for the third time in an hour he lost the rhythm.

In a voice heavy with sarcasm, Penjor Karpo remarked, "With this noise of this drum, which is meant to symbolize compassion, you show no pity for my suffering ears, Sangay. And as for the bell, which is meant to signify the Voidness of Ultimate Content — it seems to me to signify only the great void between your ears."

And so it went. By lamplight, after the last meal of the day, they memorized the basic dance steps, and learned the chanting that accompanied them. All night in his exhausted sleep Sangay rang bells, and twisted hand-drums, and moved his feet this way and that. But there was worse to come, for now they must learn the shapes and patterns of the dances, the spinning, circling, leaping, stamping configurations in which each step, each gesture, each movement had its own symbolic meaning. Sangay's arms and legs seemed too long, too graceless for these precise and intricate movements. In all else quick-witted, in the dance he was clumsy and easily confused. Serenity, composure, confidence — the more he practised, the more these qualities eluded him. Time and again he felt the sting of the dance-master's tongue, the bite of his long thin rod. And yet, in his imagination, he danced as though his limbs were wind and fire and water. He danced, in waking dreams, as the gods were said to dance in the heavenly kingdom of Guru Rimpoche.

He saw the pattern, the tapestry of the dance, the intricate interweaving of theme and gesture, movement, colour, as one sees from a distance the wondrous design of a mandala. It was only in the midst of it all, when his feet tangled themselves up like juniper-roots, and his limbs refused to respond to the desperate urgings of his brain, that the dance lost all sense, all pattern for him.

***

Another winter came. This year had been uncommonly mild, and as the time of Tsechhu approached, the high passes, usually choked with snow in the winter months, remained open to determined travellers. Pilgrims arrived almost daily at the gates of the White Leopard Dzong, seeking shelter and a bowl of rice. And so it was that a message found its way to the Dzong from the high yak-country to the northwest — from Sangay's own village.

"I have some news for you," said Rigdzin Godem that morning, as Sangay was settling himself to his studies in a corner of his tutor's cell.

Sangay glanced up from his leaves of scripture.

"Your father and your mother send greetings to you."

Sangay felt a clutching at his heart. As often as they could his family sent such messages — with wayfaring monks, with pilgrims or wandering storytellers; sometimes even with Dzong officials. From time to time there were gifts of barley-cakes or sweetmeats; and once a pair of felt boots — much too fine for any novice to wear — which he knew his mother had embroidered with her own hands. His family had not forgotten him, nor could he imagine ever forgetting them.

"I thank you, Master," Sangay said politely, and returned to his scriptures.

"But there is more to the message. Look up, boy, pay me a little attention — or don't you wish to hear?"

At once Sangay lifted his eyes to Rigdzin Godem's face.

"Your mother says that if the passes remain open, she will come to visit you at Tsechhu."

Sangay gaped at his teacher. His heart had begun to hammer like a dragon-drum. This was a thing he had dreamed of, but had never dared hope might happen.

"And my father, too?" he managed to ask. "And my brother, and my little sister?"

"This was the briefest of messages, brought by a pilgrim — you are asking me for a book of scripture." Though Rigdzin Godem's speech was as abrupt as ever, his stern face had softened a little. "However, I gathered it is to be your mother, only, and your brother."

Sangay nodded. There was a great lump in his throat, a sudden, inexplicable stinging behind his eyes. "Of course," he said. "Someone must stay at home to tend to the herd."

His mind raced ahead. The dance — he must master the steps of the Dance of Gods and Demons. Somehow he must make his hands and his limbs obey, must overcome their stubborn, wilful awkwardness. Somehow, by Tsechhu, he must acquire the grace and skill that had so long eluded him.

If he practised hard, skipped meals, shirked chores, missed sleep, crept back to the practice-hall when no one was there, then surely he could manage it. It was purely a matter of discipline, of control, the mastery of the mind over muscle, bone and sinew — how often had Penjor Karpo told him that? He could do it, must do it. When his mother and Norbu watched the Dance of Gods and Demons they would cry out in amazement to see him as a wizard, black-hatted, gorgeously apparelled. Or maybe he would be an animal-headed demon, leaping and capering, and Norbu would shout with laughter at his brother's comic tricks. His heart leaped at the thought of it.

***

Gungbar Wangyal, the First Dancer of the White Leopard Dzong, had retired in the spring, and it was Wanjur, this winter, who would dance the part of Guru Rimpoche at the New Year's Festival. The Wizard Chief was chosen, and the Bull-Headed Lord of Death; then it was time for the dance-master Penjor Karpo to choose the other dancers — the wizards, demons and death-spirits. Sangay watched and held his breath and said a silent prayer as one by one the sorcerers' parts were taken. He knew in his heart he would not be chosen for any of these; the wizards' parts went, by custom, to the older, more experienced *gaylongs*. Then one by one the demon-dancers were named: those who would wear skull-masks, and those who would wear the heads of animals. One by one the young monks stepped forward, and Sangay's heart sank, for still his name had not been called. Surely, when it came to the death-spirits who began the dance — they had nothing to do but skip and caper and play the clown, and even he could be trusted to do that much without tripping over his feet or the hem of his robe. But still his name was not called, not even to be one of the *dorma* guards — a part reserved for the rawest acolytes, who did not dance at all but only stood shivering and bewildered in the centre of the circle.

***

Sangay crouched in the cold passageway outside the dance-floor, with his face turned against a pillar. Monks did not weep. He had shed no tears since the day that he had put on the russet robes of his vocation. Now, to his dismay, they welled forth hot and stinging, and he had no power to hold them back.

Someone touched his shoulder. Hastily he wiped his face against his sleeve. Then, red-eyed and embarrassed, he turned his head to look. Wanjur was gazing down at him, half-sympathetic, half-amused.

"Sangay, my poor friend. Does it matter so much to you?"

Sangay drew a long breath and very slowly let it out. Seeking quietness of spirit, serenity of mind, he said a mantra in his head. "It would not matter at all — except that this year my mother and my brother will be watching."

Wanjur sank to his heels so that his eyes were on a level with Sangay's. "Indeed, that makes it all the harder to wait and not be chosen. Still, as my old dance-master used to say — all monks must dance, but not all monks are dancers."

"He could have been talking about me," said Sangay, staring miserably at his feet.

"Or for that matter, Pema Lingpa." Wanjur's eyes smiled, though his face was solemn. "Pema Lingpa made dances — he didn't perform them."

"He was a dwarf," said Sangay morosely.

"And you, on the other hand, seem intent on becoming a giant. Anyway, I know you have worked hard. It was not for lack of effort, that Penjor Karpo overlooked you."

"No," said Sangay bitterly. "Only for lack of skill and talent. I told you, did I not, that I would never make a dancer?"

"I remember. And I replied, if you will recall, that with those strong shoulders and long
arms you might make an archer. I have watched
how you handle a bow, this past year. It is only
a little more instruction and a great deal of
practice that is lacking."

Sangay made no reply. Sunk in the black
depths of his misery, he did not for the moment
understand what was being offered.

"Would not your mother and your brother
like to watch the New Year's archery competition?" said Wanjur, quietly persistent.

Sangay stared at him; and, as realization
came, the dull weight in his chest eased a little.

"Admittedly," said Wanjur, "there is not a
great deal of time left. But they say that if you
are faced with three impossible tasks, the least
impossible is the one you must choose. If you
work as hard as you did at dancing, making an
archer of you may not be so impossible after
all." Wanjur stood up. "Wait here, Sangay. I
have something for you."

When he came back he was carrying a fine
bow of split bamboo. The string was made of
shredded nettle stalks, twisted and folded and
carefully retwisted. There was a quiver as well,

overplaited with bast in coloured patterns, and feathered bamboo arrows, reed-slender and metal-tipped. "This is the bow that won me the first white scarf for my belt," said Wanjur. "I was no older than you. Take care of it, and it will serve you well."

ONE WITH THE AIR
AND WIND

Whenever Wanjur had time to spare from dance rehearsals, Sangay went with him to the archery grounds. Shouldering his new bow, Sangay told himself sternly, I must not stray into the Non-Virtue of Material Attachment. As Rigdzin Godem was fond of reminding his pupils, those who held on to material things were reborn as hungry ghosts. But Sangay knew in his heart that the bow was one of his greatest treasures, second only to the boots of embroidered felt his mother had sent him.

Sangay noted Wanjur's every move, his every gesture, as the older monk drew back the bowstring, feet planted at right angles, torso bent forward and bow pointing skyward, face screwed into a grimace of fierce concentration. Sangay sent a small prayer with every one of Wanjur's arrows as it sang from the string, holding his breath as it sped down that impossibly long path to the painted wooden target. When it struck home he leaped into the air with a great whoop of joy.

Then his own turn came, and he was careful to mimic Wanjur's stance, copying the way he held his shoulders and his head, the placing of his feet and the grip of his fingers on the bow. When Wanjur shot, the whole process seemed smooth and effortless — a single, fluid, graceful motion; and the arrow flew straight for the mark. However, as Sangay had already discovered, the thing was not as easy as it looked. As he stood with arrow nocked, arms held high, nearly at full stretch, his hands trembled with effort; when he opened his fingers to loose the arrow, not only his hand and arm but his whole body jerked. Before, it had not mattered that his arrows fell short or went wobbling crazily off to one side. Now, suddenly, with Wanjur looking on, he was panic-stricken. His throat ached, still, with the bitter memory of disappointment,

of defeat. Would it always be thus? Would this
wayward, undisciplined body forever mock and
disobey him? Convinced that he was doomed
to failure, he sent his arrows spinning ever
more wildly into the air. But Wanjur did not
shout insults, or wave his fists, or strike Sangay
with a rod for his mistakes, as the dance-master
would have done. Instead, he smiled his en-
couragement, saying, "Well shot" as often as he
reasonably could, and otherwise, saying nothing.

"You must begin by breathing right," Wanjur
told him. "Set your bow aside for now — we must
begin at the beginning." And he showed Sangay
how an archer must breathe: how each action
in turn — nocking the arrow, raising and drawing the bow, loosing the shot — began on an
in-drawn breath, was sustained on a held
breath, and ended with a slow and gentle
breathing out. Gradually Sangay mastered the
trick of it; and as he learned to control his
breathing, so too did he learn to relax the stiff
muscles of his arms and shoulders and legs,
letting his two hands do all the work. But still,
each time he opened his fingers to loose the

arrow from the string, the force of recoil made his hand jerk and sent the shot wild.

"That is the last thing any archer learns," Wanjur said.

"It will come, in time." And picking up his own bow, he showed Sangay how, when the body was a willing servant to the mind, the sudden shock of release through hand, wrist, arm, shoulder, could be controlled, absorbed.

"You must let go of all thought, all purpose," Wanjur told him. "You must let go of yourself. You are one with the wide air and the wind, one with the arrow and the bow."

In time, under Wanjur's gentle tutelage, Sangay's self-confidence was restored. When Wanjur left the archery ground after one of these sessions, in a hurry as always for fear of missing rehearsal, Sangay would stay behind. Again and again, with grim determination, he took his stance and raised his bow. Every night his arms and shoulders ached, and in spite of the leather guards he wore, the pads of his fingers grew raw. Sometimes he was late for prayers, or meals, but never for his lessons with Rigdzin Godem.

***

At festival-time the families of the young monks poured through the gates of the Dzong, carrying baskets and bundles filled with gifts. Some of them had been on the road for days. The children were dancing with excitement. The fathers looked proud and a little bewildered as they gazed anxiously round for their sons. The mothers walked behind, some carrying babies. Their faces were tired and travel-worn, but filled with joyous anticipation.

Sangay's mother had not changed, though she was perhaps a little thinner than he remembered her, and there were faint streaks of grey in the sleek black of her hair. He saw, with a sudden pang of remembrance, that under her heavy fur-lined cloak and ceremonial scarf she wore the same *kira*, the same red jerkin, the same beads and silver clasps as on the day that he left home.

But surely this tall youth who walked beside her could not be the fat-cheeked toddler Norbu?

He saw the look of puzzlement on their faces as they peered from face to face, and realized that in that crowd of red-robed, crop-haired figures, his family did not recognize him at all.

"Mother!" he cried out. "Norbu!" and saw them turn to him in astonishment and joy.

His mother seized his hands and stared at him, making little noises of approval as she observed his length of limb and breadth of shoulder, the dignity of his plain monk's garb, and — most surprising of all — the new air of solemnity with which he greeted her. Could this be her little Sangay, whom she had nick-named the monkey-child for his impudence, his trickster ways? She reached up almost shyly to touch his cheek. Once she would have thought nothing of scooping him into her arms and hugging him against her breast; now she was hesitant, unsure of herself. He had moved beyond her, had become a part of this im-mense, unknowable world of ritual, and cold stone, and prayer.

"Will we see you in the Dance, my son?" she asked, in the voice one uses to address a stranger.

"Next year," Sangay replied, a shade too quickly.

She smiled, and he saw to his relief that she accepted this unworthy half-truth.

He stood awkwardly smiling at her, unable to think of anything to say. The world he had left behind seemed strangely insubstantial, the concerns of that world as remote as if they belonged to some other lifetime. But his mother did not seem to feel any need for words. After her long journey, she was content simply to have arrived. Norbu, however, was shuffling his feet and tugging the ends of his scarf with a small boy's impatience.

"Open your pack," his mother said, and Norbu reached eagerly for the ties. They had brought gifts of cheeses, butter, biscuits, dried chilis, for Sangay and for his tutor Rigdzin Godem.

Sangay could understand his brother's restlessness. For Norbu, everything here was strange and wonderful. The Dzong was the enchanted fortress of a hundred hero-tales, inhabited by gods, demons, sorcerer-priests. On this day when anyone might explore its mysterious maze of passageways and gaze upon its inmost secrets, he could not bear to waste a moment in idle chatter.

But, thought Sangay sadly, when the time comes for the greatest mystery of all, when the Great Dance begins, I will not be a part of it.

"Listen," Sangay blurted out, taking no time at all to weigh the matter, "it is two days yet 'till the Dance of Gods and Demons. Tomorrow, if you like, you can watch the archery match between the village and the monks of White Leopard Dzong."

Suddenly he had Norbu's full attention. "And you, brother? Will you be taking part in this competition?"

"Of course," said Sangay. In his own mind, at least, the matter was decided. "I will be shooting for the Dzong, and it would please me very much if you came to cheer for me."

***

Sangay was awake next morning before the first gongs sounded. In the fuzzy-headedness of waking, he could not think why he was so light-hearted — why, for the first time in weeks he was filled with this sense of eagerness, of pleasurable anticipation. Then with a rush of pure joy it came to him. Even now, in the village guest-house, his mother and his brother would be drinking their butter-tea and putting on their festival garments.

Though yesterday had been blustery and overcast, the air today was clear, the prayer-flags hanging limp against their poles. One could not have hoped for better shooting weather.

The members of the Dzong team were not chosen before the match; whoever found himself with time to spare from other duties was welcome to join in. During first prayers Sangay had placed himself inconspicuously behind a pillar, and thus, so far, had escaped the attention of the senior monks. At festival time they seemed to invent a thousand small tasks to keep the *gaylongs* at a dead run from dawn till lamplight.

He collected his bow and quiver from his small corner of Rigdzin Godem's cell. Rigdzin Godem himself was nowhere to be seen. No one questioned Sangay as he slipped through the great gates of the Dzong and made his way down the steep slope to the archery ground.

The weapons tent had just been set up, with quivers hanging on either side of the door. In a larger tent at the edge of the field the women were stirring cauldrons of butter-tea. A crowd of village folk had already gathered. The archers strutted up and down the field in their embroidered felt boots, with their short-swords thrust through their belts and bright silk feast-day vests over their *khos*. Their mothers and sisters, resplendent in flower-patterned *kiris*, silver chains and brooches, necklaces of coral and turquoise and agate, chattered on the sidelines. There were prayers and ceremonies. Flutes and drums and long-horns sounded. Some of the women began a round-dance in the middle of the field.

In the midst of this festive confusion, Sangay caught sight of his mother in her gay red jerkin, with Norbu, basket-laden, following behind. Flushed and breathless with excitement he saluted them, and bow in hand went to take his place with the *gaylong*'s team.

At that moment fat Phuntsho Zangpo came trundling across the field and bore down with fierce intent upon Sangay.

"I have been searching for you for an hour," Phuntsho Zangpo said. His brow glistened with sweat; his chest heaved under his robe. "What are you doing here, Sangay?"

"As you can see, I am getting ready to shoot." He added, unkindly, "You had better get off the field. It will be much easier to hit you, than to hit the target."

Phuntsho chose to ignore this. "You had better get back to the Dzong at once," he said. "The Senior Monk Tubten Rimpoche sent me to find you. You are needed to help cut torches for the Procession of the Butter Lamps."

Sangay placed a wordless curse on Phuntsho Zangpo's head. At any other time, he would have been happy to play even this small part in the Tsechhu rites. But on this day, of all possible days . . .

He looked up. His mother was hurrying towards him, necklaces bouncing, ceremonial scarf trailing on the breeze. Close at her heels was Norbu, trotting to keep up.

"Listen quickly," Sangay said to Phuntsho Zangpo. "There is my mother, who has brought me a whole sackful of good things to eat. All of it will be yours, if only you will do one small thing for me."

Phuntsho peered with interest at Sangay's mother. "What kind of thing?"

"Tell Tubten Rimpoche that you looked everywhere for me and could not find me."

Phuntsho's jaw dropped, and his eyes went wide. "But that is a falsehood. I will be found out. I will be beaten."

Sangay pointed out hurriedly, for his mother and Norbu were almost within earshot, "You are always being beaten anyway, for your laziness. And this time you will have biscuits and cheese to comfort you afterwards."

Phuntsho hesitated. His eyes shifted from Sangay to the basket Norbu was carrying.

"Go quickly," Sangay told him, almost shouting. "It is only a very little lie, hardly a lie at all. If you had not come all the way down here to look, you would surely never have found me."

Almost, Sangay could read Phuntsho's thoughts, as greed fought with indecision. Clearly, Sangay had no intention of returning to the Dzong. How much easier, then, to tell this small lie, quickly and easily spoken, than to attempt a tedious explanation? And a sackful of biscuits would surely be a fine thing to have hidden in one's rug on a cold winter night.

"Yes, well," said Phuntsho Zangpo. "Very well, then. Maybe I will do it. How large a sack?"

Sangay held up both hands, letting his wrists sag a little under an imaginary weight.

"You must swear never to tell anyone I saw you here."

"I swear it. If I tell, let a hundred vampire-demons drink my blood."

This dreadful oath seemed to satisfy Phuntsho Zangpo. He sighed, shrugged, turned, and made his ponderous way back to the Dzong. And then the gong sounded, and Sangay's mother and Norbu were at his side, and the match was about to begin.

THE ARCHERY MATCH

The narrow, brightly painted wooden targets sat on earthen platforms at either end of the field. Each pair of archers shot twice, the one against the other. When they had finished they strolled to the target end to act as markers for their team-mates, standing calmly in the line of fire on the target-ramp while the arrows whistled all around them.

The Tsechhu match between the *gaylongs* and the village youths was a centuries-old tradition of the Dzong. It dated back to that violent age of civil war and siege when every monk must be a warrior. Nowadays, it was not taken quite so seriously as other contests. When the grown men of the village competed, passions ran high, and magic spells were cast at the field's edge to influence the outcome. Today's match — with no great victories to be upheld and no hard-won reputations at stake — was chiefly an excuse for fun.

The villagers amused themselves by shouting out advice and insults and singing rude, sarcastic songs. They yelled to speed the arrows on their way, and uttered terrible curses when they veered off course.

The two teams were well enough matched. Clearly, there were no master-archers on either side — though now and again a shot would land within an arrow's length of the target and score a point, sending archers and onlookers alike into a frenzy of triumphant whoops. Any archer who managed to strike the target itself was awarded a white scarf for his belt; meanwhile, play came to a halt while the village maidens danced, and team-mates, friends, and family rushed onto the field to offer congratulations.

There was a brief flurry of excitement when one of the village boys leaped up in the middle of the field just as a monk loosed his bolt, and came within an eyeblink of being shot. The village maidens, anxious to show off their fine clothes and the dance-steps they had been practising all year, had to be chased off the field between each round. But for the most part the match was uneventful, the pairs of archers trudging endlessly from one target to the other as the hours passed, with frequent breaks for food and drink, and few points scored.

Then, in mid-afternoon, a gusty wind sprang up, buffeting the tents and whipping the flags and banners around their posts. There were groans from both sides. Sangay and his team-mate Dorje Karma looked at each other in disgust. "We will be here forever," said Sangay, as they watched a well-shot arrow veer off course. "Not even Jigme Llendrup could score enough points to win."

Each time Sangay's turn came, he had to fight down the nervousness that stiffened his muscles like cold winter air. He tried to make his mind as clear as water, to be aware of nothing — neither his own body nor his mother's anxious presence, nor the shouts and jeers of the onlookers — so that the arrow slipped smoothly and effortlessly from the string. But each time his hand jerked, or a cross-wind came up, or his fingers slipped, or the arrow — perfectly released — halfway to the target developed a mind of its own, as though some demon's hand had seized it in mid-air.

The long day dragged on. Sangay's mother opened her bamboo basket, and whenever there was a lull sent Norbu onto the field with rice-balls and buckwheat bread. From time to time the village women came round with buckets of tea.

Now the light was beginning to fail. As night approached the wind dropped, but the air grew sharp. The archers were tired; their muscles ached, their hands were blue with cold.

And then they came to another round, and the villagers needed only one more point to win, and again it was Sangay's turn. With one good shot, he could win the day.

He had never in his life wished for anything as he wished, at that moment, for the arrow to fly true. But therein lay the danger. How often had Wanjur warned him of this moment, which comes to every archer, when everything hangs on a single shot, and the mind, which should be aware of nothing, as empty and purposeless as the wind, fixes itself instead on the action of the shoulder, the arm, the hands, the fingers — and all is lost.

Sangay stood for a long time in the fading light, his bow at rest, breathing quietly in and out as he had been taught. Dimly, as in a dream, he was aware that a perfect silence had fallen across the field. At last he nocked the arrow, raised the bow, and again he waited. In his head he heard Wanjur's quiet voice: "Be without aim. Be without purpose. Be without thought. You and the bow and the arrow are one." His hand flew open; the arrow slipped from the string. And in a moment he heard a great shout go up. At first he dared not look. Then, gazing down the darkening field, he saw that his arrow had struck the target very nearly at its centre, and the *gaylongs*'s team had won the day.

Sangay heard the wild howls of delight from his fellow monks, the good-humoured groans and curses of the villagers. He watched his team-mates perform their slow and graceful dance of victory, bows held out at arms length, circling and recircling in the middle of the field. As his mother and Norbu looked on, beaming with pride and half dancing themselves in their excitement, he tucked the white victor's scarf into his belt.

***

Rigdzin Godem's face was hard and unfor-
giving. "Recite for me, if you please, the Steps
of the Eightfold Path."

Sangay stared at the ground. "Right Understanding," he began. "Right Thought. Right
Speech. Right . . . " his voice faltered.

"Continue, please," said Rigdzin Godem.

"Right Conduct." Sangay shifted miserably
from foot to foot. "Right Livelihood, Right
Effort, Right Mindfulness, Right Concentration."

"Well," said his tutor, "the words slip easily
enough from your tongue. Yet we both know it
is your head speaking, not your heart. This day,
you have strayed a long way from the path.
Where was the Right Understanding, which is
free from delusions and self-seeking? Where
was the Right Thought, the high and worthy
aspirations? Today you aspired only to worldly
acclaim, which is all delusion. And Right
Speech — was it right speech to ask Phuntsho
Zangpo to lie for you? Right Conduct, or Right
Livelihood, that you should evade your duty,
and let another monk risk punishment on your
behalf? Right Effort? Right Mindfulness? Right
Concentration? Truly, it grieves me to see how

you have offended against every Step of the Middle Way."

Never in his life had Sangay felt so utterly ashamed. He attempted no reply. No reply was expected of him.

"The punishment prescribed for such an act," said Rigzdim Godem, "is that you should prostrate yourself on the steps of the chanting-hall, so that every monk who goes in to pray must step across you, and be witness to your disgrace."

Something cold and terrible clutched at Sangay's heart.

Rather let me be stricken dead, he thought. Now, at this moment, let me fall lifeless at Rigzin Godem's feet. Aloud, he said, "I beseech you, Master, only wait until my mother and my brother have departed. Then I will gladly lie on the steps of the chanting-hall — for the rest of my life, if you wish it."

"No," said his tutor. Though the hard set of his mouth might have softened just a little, his voice remained stern. "No, I do not wish that. It is a punishment meant to teach humility, and a day will serve as well as a lifetime. Neither do I wish to shame you before your family. But still, you have been wilfully disobedient, and there must be a price paid. You will not take part in the festival. You will not watch the Dance of Gods and Demons with your mother and your brother. Instead, you will stay here, in my cell, with neither food to eat nor butter-tea to drink, and with no fire to warm you; and you will pray, and meditate, and consider the error of your ways. I expected better of you, Sangay; you have disappointed me, and made me ashamed. And if you stray so far from the Middle Way again, I shall not be so merciful."

Sangay did his penance, shivering in the raw damp of the unheated cell, turning the leaves of the scriptures with stiff blue fingers, chanting his prayers with chattering teeth, while hunger, like a small fierce animal, gnawed at his belly. All the while he could hear the drums and the cymbals, the wondrous eerie music of the great brass horns.

His mind should have been perfectly calm and empty, like a still pond into which the syllables of his mantra dropped one by one like shining jewels. Instead, it was filled with all the bright, swirling, shifting colours, the noise and excitement and mystery of the Dance. And when the festival was over, when his mother, wiping her tears with the loose end of her scarf, had said her farewells and returned with Norbu into the hills, when the black hats of the wizards and the gorgeous demon-costumes had been put away for another year, he found he could not settle into the quiet, changeless rhythm of the Dzong. A restlessness, a feverish discontent had seized him. The high walls of the Dzong, in whose sheltering strength he had once taken comfort, now seemed to lean in upon him, so that he felt trapped, imprisoned. When he tried to read the scriptures, the elegant black figures danced upon the page; when he should have been meditating, dance music throbbed and pounded in his head. He performed his daily chores in half-hearted fashion, leaving floors half-swept and shrines half-dusted, letting cauldrons boil dry and fires go out. Time and again in the chanting-hall, he felt the sharp sting of the *chostimpa*'s rod upon his legs. In the corridors of his mind, all the learning he had taken so much time and trouble to acquire seemed hidden away behind locked doors.

"You showed promise once," Rigdzin Godem said. "It grieves me, to see how you persist in this wrongheadedness." And Sangay — in trouble again for the third time in the space of a day, with a heart that felt shrunken and dry as a cake charred in the fire — stared at his feet, and said nothing.

"Look at me, Sangay," said Rigdzin Godem. Reluctantly Sangay met his teacher's eyes. He had expected anger. These last months he had grown accustomed to anger, as one grows accustomed to cold and discomfort and lack of sleep. It no longer had any power to disturb him. But what he saw in Rigdzin's eyes, instead, was sadness: a kind of quiet grieving, as though some valued thing had by accident been lost or spoiled.

"I cannot tell you what to do," said Rigdzin Godem. "You must find your own way. We have shown you one path to take, but if you do not wish to follow it, that is your choice. You are free to leave the Dzong, to return to your family, if you so desire."

For a moment Sangay was overwhelmed by a homesickness so fierce that he did not trust himself to speak. To return to the hills, to the high pastures, to his parents' hearth . . . his throat ached, and he felt on the edge of weeping. Seeking stillness of mind, tranquility, he drew a long, slow breath.

He thought, I am no longer a yak-herd; I am a monk. Not a very good monk, to be sure, but still there was a time that I worked hard, was clever at my lessons, and imagined I was happy here. He thought of the pride in his mother's face, when first she saw him in the russet robes of monkhood. How could he shame her, now, before all the women of the village? How could he shame his father, and Norbu?

"Master," he said, his voice rough-edged and shrill with anguish, "I cannot tell what I must do. All the ways are closed to me. There is no path for me to follow."

It was a moment before Rigdzin Godem replied, and when he did, his voice was unexpectedly gentle.

"Once," he said, "a long time ago, I came to the same place that you are standing now. It seemed to me that I was poised on the edge of a bottomless black gorge, with no way forward and no way back; and I was filled with despair."

"But now you are here. You found your way."

"In time, Sangay. I did not find it soon, or easily. I chose to leave the Dzong, to enter a place of retreat, a hermitage, and there for three months, alone and in silence, I meditated — until at last I saw my path lying clear before me."

"And that is what you would have me do, Master?"

"I? Who am I to tell you what you must do? You must do anything you choose, or nothing. I am only remarking on what I did, in the same circumstance."

"It was a good choice," Sangay said. "It is what I will do also." And having made his decision, he felt suddenly and strangely light of spirit, as though he had been eased of some terrible burden.

Visions in the Dark

Spring returned to Druk-yul. The hills were covered with fresh green grass, and in the valley-bottoms the willow trees were in bud.

On the day after Full Moon Feast a young monk came to fetch Sangay to the hermitage, two days' journey to the north. As the great gates of the Dzong swung closed behind him, Sangay felt in his breast a kind of loosening and melting, as though his spirit, ice-bound through that long winter, were breaking free at last.

They left the pleasant valleys, the green slopes of the hills, and wound their way northward through ravines and rhododendron forests, over swinging iron-chain bridges with blackness falling away below. Late in the second day they came to the foot of a grim, dark mountainside. The hermitage clung like a cluster of lammergeyers' nests to the rocky ledges on its barren flank.

At the top of a winding path Sangay could see a *chorten* and a cluster of prayer-flags. The lama in charge of the hermitage came down the path to meet them — a tall man with quiet eyes and a grave, gentle face. In silence, he led Sangay to the place that was to be his home for the next one hundred days.

A small, dark cave had been carved into the side of the mountain, at the top of steep stairs; the front was closed in by a wall of stones and a door of rough-hewn boards bound together with bark. Within was a small fireplace in the middle of the floor, a sleeping rug, a narrow table or shelf made from a board set up on flat stones, and an altar. Nothing more.

In the darkening air of evening Sangay stood alone at the entrance to his cave. Above him, gaunt, ice-seamed crags rose black against the sky. Below, a scree-covered slope, dotted with grey-green clumps of thyme, plunged down to a narrow ledge, then dropped precipitously away. Westward, at the mouth of a high valley, ice-fields gleamed rose-red and gold where the last light touched them. He could hear a distant crashing of water on stone; there was no other sound.

He knew he was not really alone. There were other caves nearby, and if he looked far down the slope he could see the huddled roofs of storehouses and kitchens. Yet how easy it was to imagine that he was the only living soul on this vast bleak mountainside. He found the sensation exciting, and strange, and terrifying.

After the first day he saw no one, spoke to no one. Each day his single meal was left outside his door. He never saw who put it there. The food, which was usually served cold, seemed meagre and dull after the ample Dzong meals. There was plain rice, butter-tea, a little hard wheat-bread, a few tasteless vegetables — no chilis, and never a scrap of meat.

Day after day he huddled in his sleeping rug by the small fire. Though he had asked for a blanket to hang over the window, he could not keep out the cold wind that even in this late spring weather blew ceaselessly through the door-cracks. If he wished, he could walk upon the mountainside, though he had been warned not to venture too far, for fear of encountering the demons that infested the higher slopes.

Still, he had enough to occupy his hours, and gradually the world outside his cave ceased to interest him very much. He was here, after all, for one purpose only: to look into the state of his own soul. The lama had given him five subjects for contemplation: firstly, the great privilege bestowed on him, in receiving spiritual instruction; secondly, the impermanence of life, and thirdly, the cause and effect of karma; fourthly, the understanding of suffering; and finally, the necessity for spiritual devotion. And he had embarked as well upon the introductory steps which prepare a monk for spiritual development: the hundred thousand full prostrations, the hundred thousand recitations, and the hundred thousand symbolic offerings.

And so the silent hours slipped by, while his lips recited the mantras, his hands and body made the ritual gestures, and his mind roamed free, seeking paths where he had never walked before.

At the end of sixty days — though it might have been six days, or six hundred, for all that

Sangay was aware of time's passage — the lama visited Sangay's cell. He settled himself cross-legged on the dusty floor, and turned to Sangay with a gentle, unworldly gaze. "My son," he asked, "have you found the path you have been seeking?"

Sangay's lips felt stiff and clumsy from disuse. "I look into the embers of the fire," he said, "and I am reminded of my old life. I long for the high yak-pastures, and for my own hearth."

"You have not learned to let go of self," the lama replied. "Until that happens, you will be bound to this world — to home, and family, and hearthside. Those things will tug at your soul, as the string in the hand tugs at the kite. The kite cannot choose of itself to soar free into the upper air, to go where the wind takes it. As long as a hand holds the string, it is tied to earth."

"I have prayed," Sangay said, "and I have meditated. I have performed many recitations, many full prostrations, many symbolic offerings. Still I cannot see what path to choose."

The lama was silent for a moment. Then he said, "It is summer now. The sun is warm upon the mountainside. You have no need of a fire. If the things of this world bind you to this world, then let us cut those strings. Let us take away the light."

And he took Sangay to another, smaller cell, carved deep into the mountain's flank. It was as though Sangay had stepped from bright summer into the empty dark beyond the stars. There were no furnishings of any kind, only the stone floor and rough stone walls. No faintest sound reached him from the outer world. Even the air-chimneys and the food-hatch were curtained over to keep out any glimmer of light.

In the absolute dark and silence of that place, there was no longer any difference between night and day. Sangay listened to the sighing of his own breath, the drumbeat of his heart, the singing of his blood; he watched shapes and colours swirling behind his lids. Sometimes he slept, though his sleep was strangely without dreams. It was in his waking hours that the visions came.

At first they were no more than shifting colours, or a kind of vague sourceless light that flickered and danced above his head. Then one day, or night, he opened his eyes after a long sleep to discover that every shape and object in his cell — the edge of the door, the cup which

he had set down half-empty, a stone outcrop-
ping part way up the wall — was outlined with
an eerie ice-white radiance. The glow faded
after a moment or two, and once again he was
wrapped in darkness, soot-black and stifling.

On another occasion the entire cell was
flooded with a luminescence that flowed like
mist or smoke from the walls, the roof, the
floor. For a while he basked in that light, as
once he had basked in sunshine; then it too
faded, seeping into the stones like rain into soft
earth.

One day it seemed to him that vines and
flowers had begun to grow in a wild tangle over
the walls and ceiling, turning his cell into a
summer bower. He could almost smell the
heavy sweetness of their perfume. Then, as he
sat gazing at this new marvel, the walls of the
cave themselves grew thin as gauze, revealing
distant landscapes, stranger and more beautiful
than any temple-painting. In that dream-coun-
try were gardens of saffron and sandalwood,
orchards of amber and coral fruits: pavilions
of silk and crystal in meadows of lush grass the
colour of a peacock's throat. And in the farthest

distance, jewelled roofs of palaces glittered above high golden walls.

Now, in his vision, Sangay rose and drew aside the veil that fluttered between his own dark world and this shimmering, jewel-coloured land; and gathering all his courage he stepped through, into sunlight fierce as the white fire at the heart of ice. A broad road of some pale shining stone stretched out before him, and he knew he could neither sleep nor rest till he discovered where it led. But then he looked up and saw, rising above the meadows and gem-encrusted woods, a wall of mountains shrouded in mist and heaped with snow, a barrier of ice and rock so immense that surely not even an eagle could fly over it; and thinking his journey must end here, his heart sank.

At that moment a gust of wind seemed to lift him, carry him aloft. He felt himself floating like a leaf, a scrap of windblown silk. Filled with astonishment and joy, he laughed aloud, and his laughter flew away into the thin bright air like a flock of birds. He swooped, and soared; like an eagle he looked down on the jagged ice-bound peaks, the black gorges filled with serpent-mist, the snow-ranges that marched unbroken to the world's edge.

Below him lay circles within circles of mountains, and within those circles, a country patterned by ranges and rivers into a great eight-petalled lotus flower. And far, far below, he could see the lights of cities, shining like stars among the peaks.

Then — not knowing how he came there — he found himself in a room that was fragrant with incense of sandalwood, and more splendid than any temple of the Dzong: a royal hall, with pillars and beams of coral and pearl and zebra-stone, and carpets and cushions of silk brocade. In the centre of the room was a golden, gem-encrusted throne, supported by eight golden lions. An old man sat upon this throne, clad in the rich garments of a king. His cloak was of scarlet and turquoise silk, his tunic of emerald embroidered with gold. On his feet were jewelled slippers with curling toes; coral and silver and amber hung at his throat, his wrists, his ears. Yet, under all that splendour, how tired he looked, how frail and ill. His head was sunk upon his breast in sleep; the long wisps of his beard straggled down like moss on

an ancient tree. Even his silken robes were torn
and in disarray, the bright jewel-colours faded
and dull.

Now Sangay could hear music — the rumble of long horns, the insistent pulse of drums
— and he knew that a dance was about to begin.

The trumpets bellowed, and an army of
cannibal-demons, half-man, half-beast, wearing antlered masks, leaped into the room.
Prancing, cavorting, flapping their hideous
wings, they moved in ever-narrowing circles
towards the throne. Still the king slept on. His
eyelids flickered, as though strange dreams
stirred behind them; his hands moved feebly in
his lap, but he did not wake.

With a triumphant blare of trumpets, the
hero-dancers appeared: tall fierce warriors in
pleated robes, dark blue as the evening sky,
heads crowned with the Rings of Knighthood,
bearing swords, and bucklers covered with rhinoceros skin. To the beat of drums they leaped
high into the air with their thrusting swords,
scattering the demon-forces, driving them back
to the walls and trampling them ruthlessly under their booted feet.

Then, just as victory seemed near, another horde of demons appeared as though from nowhere, dropping from the roof-beams, leaping from behind pillars, pouncing out of the shadows at the far corners of the room. By force of numbers, by sheer malevolent energy, they overwhelmed the king's warriors, who fought long and bravely, but could not hold them back. Black-winged and horned and scowling, the demons crowded closer round the sleeping king.

But even as Sangay watched, breath held in horror, the scene before him wavered, flickered, the figures of the dance altering in the random, unexpected way of dreams. He saw a demon with a horned half-human head and lion's body tearing at the king's throat with its monstrous teeth. He saw a bird with enormous eagle's wings swoop down to fasten his talons in the lion's neck. And suddenly the room itself had vanished, walls and roof opening out, dissolving. He stood at the edge of a vast battlefield, where barbaric armies fought hand to hand with legions of lamas and warrior-monks, and ranks of cavalry charged across the plain on horses grey as stone. Now, instead of the

sound of horns and drums, the air was filled
with howls and battle-cries, the clatter of
hooves, and the rumble of golden chariots
drawn by war-elephants. And for one brief instant, as the illusion began to fade and the stone
walls of his cell closed round him, Sangay saw
a gigantic cloud-shadow falling across the land
— a writhing, coiling, serpent shape, whose
breath was fire and whose passage shook the
earth like thunder.

***

Day after day Sangay sat brooding in the
muggy darkness of his cell. Forgetting to eat,
unaware of his body's needs, he strove, through
endless prayer and meditation, through sheer
effort of will, to recapture the fading memory
of his vision. In the end, half-starved, exhausted, he remembered that when the kite
string is cut, the kite must sooner or later tumble back to the earth.

Some stray wind of the universe had for an
instant blown aside the veils between the worlds,
showing him a sign, a message, cryptic as the
faded letters on a prayer-wall. Through no effort
of body, or mind, or will could he interpret that
message, any more than Pema Lingpa, in the

manip's story, could read the ancient writing of the gods. Then he remembered how the Cloud-spirits had spoken to Pema Lingpa. "Sleep," they had said. "In the morning all things will be made clear."

For a night, and a day, and another night Sangay slept; slowly his weary mind and body healed themselves, and his spirit grew calm. When at last he woke, every muscle in his body was cramped and aching; but his mind was at rest, and his head was clear of visions. Rising, stretching, yawning, he seemed to hear, in the darkness, Wanjur's quiet voice: "Be without aim. Be without purpose. Be without thought." He felt as he had on that day of the archery match, when his hand flew open, and the arrow, slipping of its own accord from the string, flew straight to the mark. It was as though in his long exhausted sleep the Cloud-spirits had come, as they had to Pema Lingpa, and filled his mind with knowledge. For at last he saw his path before him, as clearly as if a great light were burning in that pitch-black cell. Of all the monks of Druk-yul, the gods had chosen him, the yak-herd Sangay, for this great purpose now suddenly, astonishingly, revealed to him.

He must set out upon a journey to this unknown land beyond the farthest snow-peaks.
Like holy Pema Lingpa he would become a
traveler in the Visionary Lands — a Treasure-
Seeker. Like Kunga Gyaltshen, he would witness the True Dance of the Gods, and return
with it to the world of men.

SANGAY'S QUEST

Sangay's hundred days of solitude had come to an end; in soft late summer sunlight he returned to the Dzong. Nothing had changed in the long months of his absence. Nothing had changed, in the White Leopard Dzong, since the day — surely a hundred lifetimes distant? — that he had first stepped through its gates. And yet, as he sat drinking his butter-tea amid the familiar hum of prayer and the soft pattering of bare feet on stone, he knew that from this day onward, nothing would ever be the same.

A wide-eyed novice approached Sangay, gazing at him with wary curiosity. "When you have finished your tea," the novice said — as respectfully as if Sangay had been a Superior Monk — "the Abbot wishes to see you in his rooms."

The Abbot sat crosslegged on his cushioned dais, wearing a fur-lined robe over his silk robes of office. He was an old man, with thin bones that even in late summer must feel the cold. Sangay had never before entered the Abbot's private rooms. With the one quick glance that courtesy allowed him, he observed a splendid confusion of objects: paintings, silk hangings, banners, Buddha images, a fine *chorten* of gleaming brass, numerous chests and small tables and cabinets of carved wood, and on the far wall, a wonderful display of ancient weapons — shields, helmets, lances, scimitars from long-ago battles.

Sangay stared down at the silk-carpeted floor. His apprehension grew as he waited for the Abbot to speak. Even in solitary retreat, had he contrived to commit some new and grievous error?

But there was no anger, no reproach in the Abbot's voice as he said, "My son, it gives me pleasure to see you safely returned. You were often in my thoughts, these hundred days; and I wish to know, now, if you found the answer you sought."

Sangay hesitated for the space of several long breaths.

"Honourable One, I did not find the thing that I was sent to find."

"And what was that, my son?"

Sangay fumbled for words. "A simple answer to a simple question."

The Abbot smiled. "The most difficult of all quests," he said dryly. "And what was the question?"

"Whether to remain here, to live out my days as a monk, or whether to return to my father's house."

The Abbot waited patiently for him to continue. Under that mild uncritical gaze, Sangay's nervousness began to ease a little.

"Honourable One, I discovered the road that I must take — and it is neither of those, but a third path, a high and dangerous road over many mountains, into unknown lands."

He struggled to shape into words the fragile substance of his dream. Never had ordinary speech seemed so clumsy, so inadequate. He spoke of the great room, with its pillars of coral and pearl and zebra-stone, and of the frail and ancient king who slept on the golden lion-throne. He sought to describe the intricate steps of the hero-dance, and the mad cavorting of the cannibal-demons. But even those vivid details, that he had thought forever engraved upon his mind, had begun to elude him; and when he tried to speak of the last and strangest figure of the dance — that vision of godlike armies clashing against a vast backdrop of earth and sky — he could find no words, and lapsed, defeated, into silence.

"I have never seen such a dance," said the Abbot; and hearing those words so calmly and dispassionately spoken, Sangay could have wept with shame. How could he have dared to waste the Abbot's time with such foolishness? How could he have imagined that like the saints and holy sages — like Kunga Gyaltshen, like Pema Lingpa — he had been granted some mystic revelation? He was no sage, and certainly he was no saint.

"But neither," continued the Abbot, "did I see with my own eyes the Drum Dance of Dramitse as Kunga Gyaltshen beheld it for the first time in the heavenly palace of Guru Rimpoche. Few of us, in any age, have been permitted to see the dances as the gods themselves perform them; and fewer yet have returned to teach those dances to mortal men."

Hope stirred suddenly in Sangay's breast. "But Honourable One, could it have been a true vision I saw, or was it only a waking dream?"

"What is life," said the Abbot, "but a waking dream? At this very moment, Sangay, I am dreaming you into existence, as you are dreaming me. That this life is real, that we sit in this room, that we speak these words, is a shared illusion. Yet it is also a version of the truth."

"And my dream?"

"Is another illusion — and another version of the truth."

"Then tell me, Honourable One, what I must do."

"No," said the Abbot gently. His face was the benign, impassive face of a Buddha-image. "I can tell you nothing. I can only repeat to you your own words, which you seem already to have forgotten. You have found your path, Sangay — your high and dangerous road, over many mountains. And you have already set your feet upon it."

BOOK TWO

THE ROAD TO SHAMBHALA

THE SORCERESS

Sangay paused at the top of a ridge long enough to catch his breath and rub the cramped muscles in his calves. He wiped his hot, wet face against his sleeve, sighed, and started downhill again.

For three days he had followed this narrow trail as it climbed through high cloud-forest. His robe clung to his skin in the humid air, his feet were sore, his knees ached; and for the first time since setting out, he felt the stirrings of fear.

The mist, that all morning had hung in the upper air like a pale haze, was beginning to close in, and the last of the watery light was fading. Streamers of lichen brushed against his face like long damp fingers; tangled clumps of tree roots clogged the path. The air smelled of rain-wet flowers and leaf-mould.

He walked slowly, feeling his way step by anxious step over moss-covered stones and a litter of orchid-blossoms, while the darkness deepened, and the mist folded itself around him. Somewhere in the underbrush there were slitherings and chitterings, and now and then an ominous low grumbling. Every unexplained noise sent his heart jolting into his throat. He had been warned of bears and yetis in these mountain jungles, and who knew what ghosts and demons made their homes in the shadows beside the path?

"*Om mani padme hum,*" he chanted softly, and took his travel-bow out of his pack.

The path rose before him, root-buttressed like a staircase, dangerously steep. With the last of his strength he scrambled to the top. Pushing his way through a bank of ferns, he found himself at the edge of a high meadow covered with thorn and matted clumps of juniper. Beyond, to the northwest, rose lofty snow-peaks, rose-tinted in the evening light.

It was a wild, lonely place, with not so much as a prayer-flag or a heap of mani-stones to mark a travelled path. But then, far across the tableland, black against the last rays of the sun, Sangay glimpsed a solitary, swiftly-moving figure. It ran upright, like a man, and its shape was human enough, yet so rapidly did it cover the ground that Sangay thought it must be a spirit of some kind, a ghost or demon. He looked desperately around for somewhere to hide, but on this bleak plateau there was no tree, no rockfall, not so much as a rhododendron bush to give him shelter.

The figure approached with a peculiar bounding gait, barely touching the earth with the balls of its feet, then springing high into the air like a great bird unfurling its wings. As it moved nearer, Sangay gave a sigh of relief, for its face, like its shape, was clearly human.

Whoever this strange traveller might be, he seemed unaware of Sangay's presence. His wide unblinking gaze was fixed, instead, on an invisible point in the upper air. Sangay did not dare to call out a greeting. He had heard tales of the *lung-gom-pas* — sorcerer-lamas who travelled at astonishing speeds, with neither rest nor food, across enormous distances. Clearly, this was a *lung-gom-pa* deep in trance, and to break his concentration might injure or even kill him.

The runner bounded serenely past, then gradually slowed his pace. Some distance further on, he glided to a halt. With a faintly puzzled air, like a sleepwalker waking in a strange place, he turned and looked back. He raised one hand in greeting, then beckoned impatiently to Sangay as though urging him to catch up.

Sangay raced after the sorcerer. Loose stones bruised his feet; his shoulders ached. He paid them no heed.

"Ogyay! Ogyay!" said the runner. "You are taking trouble." It was one of those pleasant, pointless greetings exchanged by travellers, and spoken as casually as a senior monk might greet an acolyte, encountering him in the courtyard of the Dzong.

Sangay realized, suddenly, that this odd stranger was a woman. It was easy to see why he had been mistaken. She was very tall, even for a man: broad-shouldered, long-limbed, with the proud, erect bearing of a warrior-monk. Sangay peered curiously up at her. Impassively she returned his stare. Her eyes, set slantwise in

a lean, sharp-angled face, were black as the
shadows at the bottoms of ravines. Her hair
seemed at one time to have been plaited, but it
had long since escaped and now hung to her
waist in a black, tangled mass. She had chopped
it into a ragged fringe across her brow, and over
it wore a peculiar hat of felted yak-hair, with five
points that stuck out around her head like tails.
On one ear-lobe was a cluster of small bright
bird-feathers; from the other there dangled a
shoulder-length bauble of amber, coral and
turquoise. She wore, as well, three or four necklaces made of coral beads and small pieces of
grey bone. There were silver rings on her fingers, and dozens of silver bangles on her wrists.
From a chain at her waist hung various charms
and amulets, a number of small skin pouches,
cooking-pots in several sizes, and a magic knife,
a *phurba*, in a fine embroidered case. A wolfskin
cape was tossed jauntily over one shoulder;
beneath it Sangay glimpsed a shirt of soiled
yellow silk, and a dark red jerkin. Round her
calves clung a long limp skirt that might once
have been white but was now an indeterminate
shade of grey; beneath that were skin leggings,
and a ragged pair of embroidered boots.

"Well?" the woman said irritably, "have cannibal-demons eaten your tongue? Where do you come from, Little Monk, and where are you going?"

Not so little, he thought indignantly; he would soon be sixteen — a man, by anyone's reckoning. Though it was true that when she drew herself up to her full height this sorcerer-woman stood head and shoulders above him.

He said, with dignity, "I have not yet found my path."

She gave a hoot of laughter. "A lost pilgrim — well, to be sure, there are plenty of those wandering the hills. Sooner or later the wolves get them." Her voice was low-pitched — more like a man's voice than a woman's — with a kind of rasp in it, like a gate-hinge that has not been oiled for a long time.

"I have a destination," Sangay assured her. "But now I must discover the true path that leads there."

She grinned. "Well then, for all you know, your feet may be set upon it — shall I come with you, Little Monk?"

He looked up at her in surprise, and then realized how fiercely he had hungered for companionship — even the companionship of this wild woman, who could as easily be a brigand as a sorceress, and might use her *phurba* to slit his throat.

"How shall I keep pace with you? I have no training in the magic arts."

She shrugged one fur-clad shoulder. "So? I run with the wind when it suits me. This morning it suited me. Maybe now it suits me to stump along at your side like a three-legged dog."

Sangay laughed in spite of himself. "And what may I call you?"

"Jatsang," said the woman, grinning good-naturedly under her ragged fringe of hair. She turned, and without looking to see whether Sangay followed, set out at a brisk lope across the stony plain.

He caught up, and they walked side by side in a companionable silence. Sangay could just keep up with the woman if he set his mind to it, matching her long, loose-jointed stride and the regular slow rhythm of her breathing. He fell after a while into a kind of half-trance, so that his fatigue vanished and he felt he could go on walking all night.

In an hour or two they had reached the
tussocky slopes at the mountain's foot. By now
it had grown too dark to travel safely. The moon
was veiled in mist, and cloud cover hid all but
a scattering of stars. Somewhere not far off
wolves howled.

"Let us find ourselves a cave," said the
sorceress. "We will have a fire, and some sup-
per, and spend the night in comfort."

She moved off up the mountainside and
vanished behind a ridge. A moment or two later
she was shouting down to Sangay. He scrambled after her, his feet slithering on scree. She
had found a shallow cave scooped out of the
base of a cliff and half-hidden by juniper scrub.
Clearly, this place had been used by other travellers. At the mouth of the cave some blackened
stones made a rough hearth, just large enough
to hold a kettle. Squatting on her heels, the
sorceress scratched some magic signs on a rock
at the cave-entrance — to keep out demons, she
said. Then she sent Sangay off into the dark to
gather fuel.

No sooner had he set down his armload of
juniper branches than the sorceress handed
him a pot from her belt and told him to look

for water. By the time he returned she had a fire blazing. Soon there was hot butter-tea in Sangay's cup, and the woman was stirring a strong broth thickened with wheat flour.

As he lifted his cup to his mouth Sangay's sleeve fell back from his wrist, and happening to glance down, he cried out in sudden alarm. Clinging to the soft flesh of his inner elbow was a long, swollen, maggot-shaped thing. It was huge, blood-gorged, black as pitch in the firelight. In panic he scraped at it with his other hand. The thing writhed and twitched, but he could not make it let go.

The sorceress glanced up, and saw him holding his arm straight out in front of him.

"What's wrong?"

"I don't know," Sangay told her. His voice was shrill with fright. "See, there's something stuck to my flesh. I think it's a vampire-demon."

The woman reached out and seized his wrist, turning his arm over so she could examine the inner side. Suddenly she laughed.

"Stupid boy, have you never seen a leech before? The wet valleys are full of them." Holding his hand firmly in her own, she twisted the squirming creature from his flesh, and before it could attach itself to her own finger she scraped it casually against a rock. Sangay looked down at his arm, and saw blood streaming from elbow to wrist. He wrapped a loose end of his robe around it. His face was hot with embarrassment. Only a leech — a trivial pest that pilgrims joked about. And he had imagined it was a demon, and had shown this sorcerer-woman that he was afraid.

"Where there is one leech, there are no doubt more," said the sorceress. "You'd better look under your clothes."

Sure enough, there were three on his left ankle, and one just above his right knee. Another had crawled up his arm and fastened itself to his chest. Two more clung to the nape of his neck. One by one the sorceress plucked them off; and then she made him take off his robe and shake it out over the fire. Blood was still pouring down his arm, and he was starting to feel a little sick. The woman mixed water with ashes, and added a pinch of herbs from one of her many pouches.

"Here," she said, handing him a strong-smelling grey paste. "Smear this on your bites. It will stop the bleeding."

After three cups of tea and two helpings of broth Sangay's stomach felt less queasy. He had had few dealings with sorcerers, and now that he was face to face with one, he wished to learn all that he could. He said to the woman, out of simple curiosity, "You are a *lung-gom-pa* — why did you not use magic to destroy the leeches?"

She looked at him with good-natured contempt. "How stupid you are," she remarked. "What did they teach you at that monks' school? Truly, I have known yaks with greater intelligence." She poked the fire fiercely with a stick, for emphasis. "Should I also use magic to pound the tea, or fetch the water, or make a fire without tinder? The arts of magic are hard-won, Little Monk, and not to be squandered for trivial purposes. You would do well to remember that."

THE WINTER ROAD

At dawn they began their ascent towards the high snow-passes. When they came to a prayer-wall at the top of a windswept ridge, Sangay saw to his surprise that the sorceress walked round it the wrong way, with her left shoulder to the wall instead of the right. Clearly, this woman was not *chos-pa* — a follower of the Great Way. She must practise the old Bon faith which prevailed in Druk-yul before the coming of the Precious Guru.

In mid-afternoon they came to a country of small lakes, stretched like a string of turquoises among steep pine-clad hills. A goat-path wandered down from the high ground to a rocky shoreline. The surface of the water was glassy smooth, a perfect blue-green mirror reflecting snow-peaks, sky and clouds.

"Look," said Sangay, staring, as Jatsang bent at the lake's edge to fill her water-jug. On a small island just offshore sat a hermit, clad only in a thin ragged length of cotton. A heavy iron chain was wrapped several times round his waist. He appeared to have no hut, no hearth-fire, no sleeping rug, no shelter or comfort of any kind — only that small bare patch of stony soil, surrounded by a glittering expanse of water. His eyes were closed, his face serene; he paid them no heed as they approached.

"Go softly," warned the sorceress. "He is deep in trance."

Setting his feet down carefully on the loose stones, Sangay craned his neck to peer at the old man. "How long has he been there?" he whispered.

The sorceress shrugged. "Who knows? Maybe always. He has lived there, summer and winter, for as long as anyone remembers."

"And how long must he remain?"

"As long as he chooses," she said. "Or until the birds pick clean his bones."

Sangay remembered the hundred days of his own retreat. He tried to imagine a whole lifetime spent in such dreadful solitude.

"And why does he have that chain wrapped around his body?"

"Because," said the sorceress patiently, "he is *lung-gom-pa*, and through the long practice of his art he has made his body lighter than the air itself. Without the chain to weigh it down, he would float away on the slightest breath of wind."

Sangay looked back at the hermit on his patch of dirt, seeing with pity and awe the frail, wasted body that having renounced all natural laws must be held down by chains, while the mind, unfettered, soared through regions of transcendent bliss. The old man had chosen the Short Path, the path of mysticism and magic — the perilous climb straight up the mountain's face, instead of the longer, slower, safer Middle Way. Sangay wondered if this was the path he himself was meant to take. And warm though the day was, a chill touched him, like cold fingers on his neck. He shivered, and walked quickly on.

And then they were climbing from summer into winter, on a sheep's track patched with ice and littered with broken stones. Hour after hour they inched their way along crumbling ledges, with ice-streaked crags rising sheer above them and the ground dropping sheer away below. When Sangay looked down he could see a river threading its way like a skein of bright green silk through the bottom of the gorge.

The track curved around a bulge in the rock-face, climbed again, and then turned sharply downward between rust-coloured cliffs. Now they could hear the roar of the river, growing louder as they descended. For a while they walked along its bank, where grey clumps of thyme pushed up through patches of fresh snow.

Around the next bend the valley narrowed to little more than a gully. At the head of the gorge, where the mountains curved in to meet one another, rose an immense barrier of ice. Sangay gazed in dismay at this unbroken white wall, flanked by its ramparts of red stone; then he sat down hard on a boulder and put his face into his hands. He could see no way to go

further, and he was too tired and discouraged
to turn back.

"What, weary already, Little Monk?" He
lifted his head. Jatsang stood across the path,
her black eyes taunting him.

"Look over there, where the trail ends. How
are we to go on?"

"As before, Little Monk, with one foot in
front of the other, and both eyes on the
ground."

"Over that wall of ice?"

"Through it, around it — mostly over it.
There is a high pass that cuts between the
glacier and the Red Mountain. Not an easy
route, but not impossible. But we must be
quick, for I can smell snow on the wind."

Even as she spoke, the sun vanished behind
thick grey clouds.

"So, are you ready, Little Monk?"

Sangay stared at the ground. He was not
ready. He was tired, and footsore, and hungry,
and he had lost all his high resolve. He wished
for a great wind, like the one in his vision, to
catch him up and sweep him effortlessly across
that icy barrier. But no, it seemed he must

trudge endlessly onward and upward, with aching limbs and feet as heavy as stones.

"Are you hungry?" asked the sorceress.

Wretchedly he nodded. "But I have eaten all my food."

"Give me your bowl."

He reached into the front of his robe and pulled out his cup. Jatsang bent, scooped it full of snow, then with a look of concentration held it tightly in her two hands. There was a faint sound of hissing. The snow in the cup melted as suddenly as though she had set it down in a bed of hot coals. Steam rose from it. She handed him the cup. It was so hot that he juggled it awkwardly from one hand to the other. The sorceress dropped in a pinch of herbs from one of her pouches. "Drink," she said.

Cautiously he sipped the tea. It had a pleasant, spicy taste, and was hot enough to sear his tongue. He blew on it to cool it, then sucked it down in three gulps. The hot tea warmed his blood, the gnawing in his belly quieted; he felt strength returning to his limbs.

"Now then," said the sorceress. Sangay observed that she herself had drunk nothing.

What hidden powers gave her strength, this woman who existed without food and drink and sleep?

She moved off at her own pace without looking back. Her feet on the ice-slick stones were as sure as a mountain cat's.

They walked on in the black shadow of the cliffs. The sky was grey and curdled-looking. Soon snow began to fall — lightly at first, then, as they climbed higher, in huge, wet, clinging flakes.

Night came. The sky was black, with neither moon nor stars, though a dim light seemed to issue from the white ground and the still-falling snow. At length they came upon a sheltered place under a shelf of rock. Huddled against the cliff-face, Sangay brushed the snow from his hair and pulled off his wet boots. He could feel the chill damp of the rocks eating into his bones. The snow fell steadily, a spinning, swirling curtain. In the wan snow-light he saw the sorceress turn to him.

"You are shivering," she said. There was no trace of sympathy in her voice.

"Is it any wonder?" asked Sangay unhappily. "I am soaked through, and my feet are like chunks of ice."

She gave a kind of grunt, as though to say, "What else did you expect?" Then she reached out a hand in the half-dark, touching his cheek. "Well, you are cold enough, that's for certain. If you spend the night in that wet robe, no doubt you'll be coughing and snuffling for days."

"Can't you make a fire?" Sangay was remembering how with a touch of her hand she had brought snow-water to the boil.

"From what? Can you find me a stick of wood, a pellet of dung?"

On his hands and knees Sangay searched the floor of their shelter. Except for a scattering of gravel, it was as bare as if it had been swept.

"There is nothing." Sangay was seized with a sudden hard shuddering. His teeth began to chatter so violently that his jaw ached.

"Stop that noise," said the sorceress. "I will show you how to keep warm."

She sat down crosslegged, passing her hands under her thighs and then clasping them together. She began to breathe very slowly and deeply, and seemed to be entering a state of trance. After a while Sangay felt a fierce warmth radiating from her, as though she were running a high fever. The heat grew and grew, until the air around her seemed to shimmer with it. Steam rose in a cloud from her wet garments. Sangay crept closer to her, as one draws near a hearth.

After a while she opened her eyes, and the intense waves of heat subsided, though she still seemed to glow with a pleasant warmth. For the first time all day Sangay felt comfortable. His boots and his sodden robe were almost dry.

"That is a useful piece of magic," Sangay said. "Will you teach it to me, Lady?" But now she growled at him out of the darkness with unexpected rancour.

"So, you think you would learn *tumo*? You who shiver and shake and turn blue with the cold, whose teeth clack like a mouthful of wind-chimes? Will you put aside your warm boots and your garment of wool, and walk naked on the mountainside in a cotton rag? Will you bathe in icy mountain streams, and then sit all night in a wet sheet that freezes on the body, night after night, from sunset to sun-up, all winter long, until you learn to make fire in your own flesh, and the frozen sheet dries on your skin, and the snow melts as it falls on your shoulders? Go, do as I did, Little Monk — learn to survive the jaws of the frozen river, the teeth of the icy gale. When you have done that, in quietness of mind and spirit, without a word of complaint, then come and ask me again to teach you *tumo*."

***

Deep in the night the wind died, and in the sudden quiet a strange cry broke into Sangay's dreams. It was a sound halfway between a wild laugh and a yelp of pain, and all the more frightening because it was so nearly human. He sat up. The cry came again, once, and then there was only the deep snow-muffled silence. The sorceress stirred, and lifted her head.

"Don't be afraid," she said. "It is only a yeti. They are night-stalking creatures — in the morning he will be gone."

"But why is he making that noise?"

"Who knows? Yetis always sound like that. Maybe it is their hunting-cry. Though my grandmother told me a story once . . . "

Sangay rubbed the sleep out of his eyes and waited. A moment before the sorceress had been snoring loudly. Now she was wide awake, and seemed in a mood to talk. Sangay had noticed that she did not sleep all night, as others did, but napped like a cat whenever the impulse took her.

"She was captured by a yeti," the sorceress said.

Sangay's eyes widened in the darkness. "Your grandmother, Lady?"

"She said so herself, on her deathbed. This was to be her second funeral, she said. And when I asked how that could be, she told me this tale. Like me, she came of the nomad folk who dwell in the mountains of the east. One day she had gone into the forest, high up at the edge of the snowline, to gather firewood. She lingered too long, and when darkness came, she could not find her way home. Then all at once she saw a dark shape among the trees, like a huge misshapen man; and before she had time to run away the creature leaped out and seized her, and stuffed her into the pouch on his back, and bore her away to his cave.

"When she woke next morning she saw the yeti sleeping beside her. He was half-man, half-monkey, she said — twice as tall as a man, twice as broad, and covered all over with hair. But what she noticed most of all were his enormous feet. The yeti had bound my grandmother's wrists with a strip of leather, and tied the other end round his waist, so that she could not run away while he slept. Each morning he untied her hands, and bound them again at night.

"For five whole months the yeti kept my grandmother prisoner in his cave, feeding her raw meat, and speaking to her in wordless grunts. Then one day my grandmother decided to make herself some shoes from the skin of a blue sheep the yeti had killed. When the yeti saw these shoes, it was plain that he admired them very much. My grandmother let him feel the fine soft leather, and examine the careful workmanship.

" 'Would you like a pair for yourself?' my grandmother asked, and to make him understand she pointed to his huge hairy feet. The yeti grinned, showing his great sharp teeth.

" 'Then,' said my grandmother, 'you must leave my wrists untied at night. The rope cuts off my circulation, and makes my fingers stiff.'

"So the yeti agreed. And my grandmother took two sheephides, one for each of the yeti's feet, and made him two enormous shoes. The task took her many days, for she double-stitched all the seams to make sure they could not come loose.

"At last the yeti's shoes were finished, and that night my grandmother crept softly out of the cave, and ran as fast as she could down the mountainside. The yeti woke, and tried to run after her, but my clever grandmother had sewn the shoes to his feet so that he could not take them off.

"No sooner had he left the cave, than the yeti began to stumble and slide. He was not used to wearing shoes, and he needed his bare toes to grip the rocks on the steep mountain path. Besides, my grandmother had rubbed the soles of his shoes with grease, so that he seemed to be running on ice. And so my grandmother escaped.

"When she returned to the black tents of our people, her family rejoiced to see her, for they had thought her long dead. Though," said the sorceress, "they might have been even happier, if they had not just finished paying the shaman for the last of her funeral rites."

THE VALLEY OF HIDDEN
TREASURES

All night the snow went on falling. At dawn, after Sangay and Jatsang had made tea and eaten a little rice, they dug their way through the drifts across the cave mouth. Then they pushed on up the mountainside, through a still, white world.

They were at a great height now. The air was thin, and so bitter cold that it seared the lungs. At mid-morning the sun came out, and for a while they climbed through a dazzling landscape of black rock, blue sky and glittering ice. Then, halfway through the afternoon, just as they were beginning to think about shelter for the night, the snow began again.

Soon everything — the cliffs, the sky, the path ahead, the black gorges below — had vanished. Sangay slid his boots gingerly along the path, feeling for firm ground. A single misstep could send him hurtling over the edge. The sorceress reached back and seized his hand, guiding him; but soon even her sure steps faltered, as the snow-wind rose and blew straight into their faces, snatching away their breath and blinding them. Sangay stumbled, caught himself; his hand slipped out of Jatsang's.

Somewhere overhead there was a loud whispering, a slithering, and then a mass of snow and loose stones came roaring down the flank of the hill, burying the path in front of him.

"Wait!" he called out, but there was no reply, only the cry of the wind among the rocks, and that too seemed muffled, made faint and distant by the snow.

Sangay floundered on through the knee-high drifts, his shoulder pressed hard against the cliff, calling out now and again to Jatsang, but without much hope. His legs and lungs hurt; the snow seemed to suck at him with a thousand white mouths, dragging him down and down.

Something, the slightest hint of a movement, made him glance up toward a ledge of
stone just above his head. There was nothing
there, only a long grey ice-patched rock. He
took another plunging step, and another, forc-
ing his way forward. All at once the rock on the
ledge twitched, moved, and sprang gracefully
down the cliff-side. Now Sangay could see
through the driven snow the long, lithe cat-
shape, the silver coat with its dark rosettes, the
blunt head, the broad white expanse of breast.

On soft, unhurried feet the snow leopard
padded towards him. Sangay cringed, his body
frozen with fear. He braced himself for the
instant when the great soft weight would plum-
met down upon him, crushing him into the
ground; when hungry fangs would rip apart his
flesh.

He opened his eyes a moment later, to feel
a warm flank pressing gently against his side,
teeth tugging on his sleeve. He allowed himself
to be half-led, half-dragged to safety.

A tall, thin, dark shape moved on the path
above him, and suddenly the sorceress was
crouched beside the snow leopard, her arms

circling the shaggy neck, her face pressed against the thick white fur.

The words she whispered into the leopard's ear were in no language Sangay had ever heard. They were like a snatch of song, an incantation. Then she looked up at Sangay and grinned. In her eyes was the delight with which one greets a favourite kinswoman, a long-absent and beloved friend.

"Ah, Little Monk," she said, "you are as white as Drolma's fur. Did you think she meant to crunch your bones?"

"The thought occurred to me," Sangay replied ironically. He was glad to find there was still a tongue in his head.

"She is my sister in spirit, this gentle beast," said Jatsang. "She knows that you are under my protection."

Now he saw that more of the great white cats had gathered around them, padding silently out of the storm. They pressed close, in a circle, then sat as motionless as creatures carved of stone and snow. They were so near that he could hear the soft snuffling of their breath.

"Have no fear," said Jatsang. "These are the Guardians of the Gate. If you are a true follower of the Precious Guru, they will not harm you."

"What gate, Lady?" He glanced nervously at the leopards. This sorceress, for all her cleverness, could not see into his heart. She could not know the pride and wilfulness that tainted it. She could not guess how far he had strayed from the Middle Way. The frosty eyes of the leopards stared at him, unblinking. One of them lashed his tail and Sangay cringed back, alarmed. They *knew*.

Thus preoccupied, he did not hear Jatsang's reply, and had to ask again, "What gate?"

She turned her head sharply and stared at him. "Why, the entrance to the hidden valley. Is that not the place you are seeking?"

Valleys hidden among the high peaks. The sacred places where Guru Rimpoche was said to have concealed his treasure. Once Sangay had dreamed of becoming a treasure-seeker, like holy Pema Lingpa. Could this gate through the glacier be the doorway to his visionary country?

He gazed up to the black crags of the summit, half-visible through the blowing snow. The female leopard, Jatsang's sister-of-the-spirit,

twitched her tail and rubbed her cheek against
the sorceress's shoulder, and then, as Jatsang
and Sangay pressed on up the mountain, vanished quietly into the storm.

All at once the wind died, and the sky
cleared, and they were climbing through a jewelled world, transfigured by the evening sun.
Every cliff and crag glittered with icicles, topaz
and emerald in the slanting light. Ice crunched
and splintered beneath their feet. Sangay
looked down and saw that the path was striped
with shimmering bands of colour — pale green,
white, sapphire blue and ruby-red. They had
come to a curtain of ice, suspended like a frozen
cataract across the trail. Sangay put up his hands
to shield his eyes from the glare of the reflected
sun.

Then somehow, in a dazzle of light, they had
passed through and beyond the ice-curtain into
a forest of spires and turrets and columns. The
air was very cold, very still, and filled with an
eerie ghost-green radiance. Sangay could hear
only the crackle of the ice under his boots, and
the faint whistling of his own lungs. His breath
hung before him like pale green smoke.

Now, as Jatsang led him deeper and deeper into the heart of the glacier, the path widened, and there were glistening open spaces among the thrusting ice-spires. The cold green light brightened, was edged with gold like the first flush of sunrise seeping into the sky. And then they had passed beyond the frozen forest and its shrouding wall of ice, and had come to the edge of a summer garden, a green and flowering valley hidden away among the snow-bound peaks.

Below them a river flowed over a bed of white stones. Along its banks were mossy pine-woods, and meadows dotted with spring flowers. They made their way down the gentler slopes, through banks of rhododendrons, sky blue, pale yellow, rose and amethyst, blooming out of season. Birds sang among the branches; clouds of yellow butterflies flew up like wind-blown blossoms. The air was heavy with fragrance: jasmine, honeysuckle, lavender, wild rose, mint.

Sangay was suddenly overwhelmed by exhaustion. He threw himself onto the moss-covered stones beside the river. His head ached and his skin burned with fever. He was as sure as he had ever been sure of anything, that he could not go another step.

"Get up," said Jatsang briskly.

Wearily, Sangay rolled his head to one side and peered up at her. He sneezed once, twice, three times, wiped his nose on his sleeve, and closed his eyes again.

"You cannot sleep here," said Jatsang.

"Why not?" Sangay propped himself awkwardly on one elbow. He had barely strength enough left to argue.

She shrugged. "Did we fight our way through the blizzard and risk our necks in the pass so you could take a nap?" She prodded him ungently with her foot. "What kind of monk do you call yourself? I have seen monks no older than you, measuring their lengths on their bellies in the middle of winter, three times round the base of the Sacred Mountain."

Sangay rubbed his eyes. They felt gritty. Every bone in his body ached.

"Then do as you like," he heard Jatsang say. The contempt in her voice stung him into action. Slowly, heavily, he pushed himself to his knees, and then to his feet.

Where the valley narrowed and the path wound close to the cliffs, they came to a pile of moss-grown boulders. Here Sangay stopped, though he could not have explained why. He recognized nothing. He knew he had never seen this place in dreams or in vision. And yet something in this valley laid claim upon him — some task or obligation, long forgotten.

"Wait," he said.

Jatsang glanced over her shoulder. "What now, Little Monk?"

"Lady, it is just as you said. I was meant to find this place. Something is hidden here, and I cannot leave until I discover it."

Jatsang turned, retraced her steps. "Yes," she said. "I thought you understood. It was no accident that you came here."

He found a stick and poked in the crevices among the boulders. He searched through the reeds at the water's edge, knelt down on the bank and stared into the river's spangled depths. He found nothing, but that sense of compulsion — of urgency — was growing stronger. Finally he turned away from the river, towards the cliff, flattening the tangle of vines and grasses that grew along its base. There, half concealed by ferns and honeysuckle, was a narrow cleft in the rock.

"Hah!" he shouted, beckoning to Jatsang.

Small stones had been tightly wedged into the opening. Sangay dug at them with his stick, and then with his knife. He scrabbled at them until his fingers bled. Finally he managed to pry the first stone loose, and after that the rest came easily. He bent forward, peering into blackness.

"Reach in," said Jatsang, behind him. "What are you afraid of?"

"Bears," he replied at once. "Snakes." He thought for a moment. "Demons."

The sorceress threw back her head and gazed at the distant peaks, as though petitioning the mountain gods for patience.

He who dares nothing, gains nothing, Sangay reminded himself. He drew a deep breath, and thrust his right hand into the gaping hole. At first it seemed empty. Then his fingers, groping over the rough stone floor, encountered something soft and yielding, a pouch or leather bag. When he grasped it and dragged it towards him, he could feel a solid weight inside.

He tugged it out into the light. It was a deerskin bag, brittle with age. He set it carefully on the ground.

"Open it," said Jatsang. Sangay loosened the frayed silk drawstring. He pulled out a leather belt with silken tassels, and then another, heavier object.

"Look, Lady," he said to Jatsang, astonished. He held up a ritual dagger, a *phurba*, with a three-sided blade and a dragon-shaped silver hilt. Drawing the bronze blade from its elaborate gold-washed sheath, he marvelled at its workmanship, its perfect balance in his hand. He could see no trace of rust or tarnish.

Jatsang had picked up the tasselled belt. "Put it on," she said. Sangay looked down at the dagger, and then, questioningly, at Jatsang. Inlaid with turquoise and coral, the *phurba* was made for a knight, an abbot, a prince of the royal court.

"I am not worthy to possess such a thing," he told Jatsang.

"Such a thing is not meant to be possessed," Jatsang replied. "But since you are the one who found it, it seems you are its custodian, for a time."

Sangay threaded the belt through the sheath loop, and fastened it round it his waist.

"Now look again," said Jatsang.

This time his searching hands discovered two skull-containers filled with gold coins.

"Put them back," Jatsang told him. "Leave them for the next treasure-seeker. We have no need of them on this journey. What else can you find?"

Now he discovered a bagful of food — red rice, buckwheat flour, chilis, some cakes of tea, strips of yak-meat, hard and dry as leather. Enough to last the two of them for many days. As well, there was a flask of potent arra liquor, which the sorceress appropriated for herself.

On the fourth attempt he found a smaller skin bag filled with zi-stones. He would have put them back, like the gold coins, but Jatsang looked pleased and said, "Take those," and so he tucked the white-etched black stones away in his robe.

Finally, he found a long, thin object tightly wrapped in parchment. It was a scroll, and when he unwound it, he found that it was covered with strange inscriptions, impossible to read. He remembered the tale of Pema

Lingpa the Treasure-Seeker, and a fierce excitement rose in him.

He gave the scroll to Jatsang to examine. Holding it awkwardly, diffidently — as though she thought it might crumble in her fingers or burst into flame — she peered at the strange black marks.

"Lady, do you think this is spirit-writing?"

She raised one fur-clad shoulder. "Why do you ask me? Writing is for monks. What I need to remember, I carry up here . . . " and she tapped her forehead with a long, dirty finger.

"Never mind," she said. "Bring the scroll. In one of these valleys there are scholars who will read it for you." And when Sangay had gathered up his treasures, she led the way out of the summer valley, loping tirelessly ahead of him, silent and soft-footed as a great, gaunt, shaggy-coated wolf.

THE *TULPA*

Beyond the flowering valley the path climbed steeply. Ahead lay a jumble of mountains — black snow-streaked cliffs and massifs heaped against a sunless sky. Next day at mid-morning they passed through a long, narrow gorge strewn with smooth stones the size and shape of hen's eggs. Sangay trudged silently after Jatsang. Though the ground was level, it was slow, hard going. The stones shifted and rolled with every step, and bruised his feet through the soles of his boots.

Jatsang strode on ahead, her feet moving over the waste of stones as easily as though she were walking on meadow-grass. Once or twice she looked back and laughed at Sangay's discomfort. "Hurry up, Little Monk, or I will leave you behind," she said. Fearing that she might be in earnest Sangay walked faster, and stumbling, banged his knees on the rocks. He got up, muttering to himself.

In this valley, time seemed to move as slowly as glaciers. Midday came and went and long hours slid by, with no change in the wintry light. The landscape grew stranger by the hour. Sangay could put no name to the wind-bent trees that clung to these gaunt cliffs, nor to the grey scrubby bushes that grew beside the path. The ragged peaks that thrust against the sky were like mountains glimpsed in fever-dreams, waking old and half-forgotten terrors. No gods but only demons dwelt in this country.

And when at last they reached the head of the gorge and passed through a narrow slit between two rock faces, there was only desert — an endless, desolate expanse of grey sand, broken stone and parched, colourless grass.

The shadows are the wrong colour, Sangay thought — though he could not remember at that moment what colour shadows ought to be. The light was strange. It had a dull, leaden look about it.

Sangay had left behind a world that was cold and bleak and often dangerous, but familiar to him and in its own way predictable. In this country beyond the glacier angles were twisted ever so subtly awry, shapes shifted when your head turned aside. The thought came to him: anything can happen in this place.

Only rarely did Jatsang look back to see if Sangay was keeping up. She simply assumed that he would be there. She is not afraid, Sangay told himself. She is as sure of herself here as when we were wandering among the flowers in the summer valley. Therefore, there must be nothing to fear.

The clouds rolled back and the sun hung in the middle of the sky, a glaring white-hot ball that sucked every drop of moisture from the air. The ceaseless wind that blew over this land was dust-laden, hot as a furnace's breath. It seared Sangay's throat, cracked his lips, swept fine grey sand into his face.

Finally, dizzy with thirst, he called out to Jatsang to slow her pace. They had come to a long pale ridge of rock that jutted into the midst of the waste like the bones of some huge animal. Jatsang knelt, poking about for a moment or two with a knife from her belt. Abruptly a thin stream of water welled up from between two rocks. Jatsang sat back on her heels as Sangay flung himself forward, thrusting his parched lips to the spring that had risen miraculously out of the dead land.

When at last he had slaked his thirst, he looked up to see Jatsang rummaging among the pouches suspended from her waist.

"Hold still," she said. And she began to smear his face with a grey salve that resembled nothing so much as oily mud. It had a foul smell, and stung when it touched his flesh, but soon he felt the taut skin of his face soften, and the soreness in his cracked lips eased.

Jatsang filled a pair of water-jugs from the spring, and they plodded on. At last they reached the desert's edge and began to climb again, into a wild region of hills. No grass, not so much as a thorn or juniper bush clung to these bleak heights; everything had been stripped clean by the ruthless scouring of the wind. Roaring down from the heights, it whipped Jatsang's tangled mane of hair behind her like a banner, and flung itself upon

Sangay as though it would tear the flesh from his bones.

The light had begun to fade, and the wind turned bitter cold. Exhausted, they sought what shelter they could beneath a shallow lip of rock. Immediately Sangay began to shiver. Jatsang, scowling down at him, said, "Now I suppose you want some tea."

Sangay nodded hopefully. Still scowling, Jatsang poured water into a cup, and brought it to a hard boil in her big, grimy hands.

Sangay had just finished his second cup when suddenly the sorceress put her finger to her lips in warning. Above the restless whining of the wind among the rocks he could hear the faint jangle of harness-bells. A moment later three men on tall black horses clattered into view.

They were dressed in tiger skin robes and gaudy vests of embroidered silk, emerald green and garnet red. From under fox-fur hats their long black hair hung down their backs. At their sides were swords encased in jewelled sheaths.

Thinking they must be knights or princes of this land, Sangay would have stepped forward to greet them had not Jatsang seized him roughly by the arm and dragged him back.

"Mind what you do," she hissed in his ear, "they are robbers, cut-throats. They will slit your throat from ear to ear and toss you to the wolves before you have time to open your mouth."

"Well met, sister," said the tall man who rode in front. His eyes were like river stones in his lean, rapacious face. "And you, little monk — what is your business here?"

Jatsang answered for them both. "We are *arjopas*, pilgrims. We seek the Incense Mountains, where the sages live." She spoke in quiet, sober tones, but Sangay could hear a bright edge of excitement in her voice.

"And has the begging been good?"

"Good enough."

"Indeed. It seems that your young companion has stuffed a great quantity of it into his robe."

"Provisions," said Jatsang vaguely. "A long journey lies ahead."

The robber-lord smiled, and unsheathed his sword. With one quick movement he slashed straight across the bulge of Sangay's robe.

Sangay stood in shocked silence, looking
down at the food, the scroll, the bag of zi-stones
— all the treasures of the summer valley —
lying scattered in the dust.

"Pick them up," the robber-lord said mildly.
Sangay bent and gathered up the zi-stones.

"Give them to me," said the robber, reaching out a leather-gloved hand. "And the
scroll."

Sangay watched his treasures disappearing
one by one into the robber-lord's saddle-bags.

And then an odd sensation — a kind of
shiver down his spine, as though someone had
touched cold fingers to the nape of his neck —
made him turn his head far enough to glimpse
Jatsang from the corner of his eye. She was
standing to one side of the path, wearing a
curiously blank expression. It was almost as if
she had fallen asleep on her feet.

"And the dagger," prompted the bandit,
when Sangay had handed over the last cake of
tea.

With that, Sangay's long habit of obedience,
of docility, vanished. He could not give up the
sacred dagger. The Guru had hidden it in the
summer valley, intending that one day Sangay

should seek it out. He knew, as surely as if someone had whispered it in his ear, that he alone was meant to guard it.

"No," said Sangay. He spoke softly — after years in the Dzong, one always spoke softly — but no one hearing him could have doubted his determination.

"Give me the knife," said the robber. The point of his sword rested a scant inch from Sangay's breast.

Sangay's heart fluttered in his throat like a trapped bird, but he did not move. Thoughtfully the robber shifted his sword-point upward, till it came to rest just under Sangay's chin. The dagger is precious, thought Sangay, as he felt the cold pressure of the blade against his throat — but is it worth dying for?

Slowly he drew the dagger from its sheath, and offered it to the bandit. With a wolfish smile the man closed his fingers on the beautiful dragon-hilt.

Then the robber's eyes widened, his mouth fell open, and he looked down in horrified bewilderment. The dagger had begun to twist and writhe in his hand as though it possessed a life of its own. Suddenly the blade whipped around, and with tremendous force wrenched the robber's wrist back upon itself. As Sangay stared in astonishment, the dagger blade drove deep into the man's left shoulder, piercing tigerskin robe, silk vest, skin, and flesh.

The bandit shrieked. Blood welled between his fingers as he pulled in vain at the dagger. Slowly he slid from his saddle and fell to the ground. There he lay curled on his side, panting with shock and pain.

But now the other horsemen were moving in on them. Sangay cursed his unpreparedness. There was no time, now, to unfold his travel-bow, much less to string it. Still, Jatsang seemed calm enough. She stood spraddle-legged, feet firmly planted, knife in hand, defying the nearest bandit to make his move. The bandits eyed her uncertainly. They too had seen the way the *phurba* had sprung to life and buried itself in the flesh of the man who wielded it. And the woman wore the white skirt and five-tailed hat of a magician.

One bandit, more nervous than the other, said, "Put Duggur on his horse, and let us be off."

"No, no," said his fellow. "We must first avenge Duggur's injury. It could be a mortal one." And he raised his sword in the air, and rode down upon the sorceress. In the midst of his horror and dismay, Sangay marvelled at Jatsang's serenity. Not so much as the twitch of a lip, the blink of an eye betrayed her as the sword came up.

And then there was something — a huge, unexpected, inexplicable something — towering up behind the bandit. One moment it was nothing more than the hint of a shape, a swirl of mist, a vague thickening of the thin grey air. And the next moment, it was real, and immense, and unequivocally flesh and blood — a knight, tall as two ordinary men, as handsome as a god, looking down on the bandits with an expression not so much threatening as curious and eager.

He wore the rings of knighthood on his head, and a long pleated robe the colour of the evening sky. In his belt was a sword of antique design, and on his left arm was a shield covered with rhinoceros skin. He reached out and with one deft movement twitched the bandit's sword in mid-stroke from his hand and threw it clattering down the mountainside. Leaning down from his great height he seized the two robber-lords by their silken scruffs, lifted them from their mounts and tossed them casually to the ground. Then he stood gazing at Jatsang, looking for all the world like an enormous, good-natured, obedient dog.

From somewhere behind Sangay came muffled moans, and the nervous stamping of a horse.

"Give back what Duggur has taken," he heard one man say, "else this sorceress will send her curses after us." With a series of small thuds the food, the scroll, the bag of zi-stones, the silver-hilted dagger, all landed at Sangay's feet. Then hooves pounded across the dusty earth, as the robbers rode off with their wounded comrade.

Finally Sangay managed to sputter, "How can this be, Lady? One minute there was no one there, and the very next . . ."

"Have you never seen a *tulpa*, a mind-phantom, made? No, I suppose not — in the Dzong, they only teach you to make tea and butter-images."

"I have heard of such things," said Sangay, tilting back his head to admire the phantom knight.

"He *is* a fine fellow, is he not?" said Jatsang. "I have not managed anything so impressive since the night I drove off a pack of wolves with thirty fire-demons. But now I suppose I'd better send him away."

"Must you?" asked Sangay, mindful of the long journey ahead.

The *tulpa* looked hopefully at Jatsang. Had he been the noble dog he so much resembled, thought Sangay, his ears would have stood up and his tail would have wagged.

"Well, perhaps not," said Jatsang, wavering. "Maybe for a day or so . . . we'll see. After all, it was no small task, inventing him."

Sangay gathered up his treasures, and they went on through the bleak dead land, the *tulpa* plodding cheerfully behind them, a vast, benign and strangely comforting presence.

THE COPPER FOREST

That night the *tulpa* crept close to Jatsang's small fire, spreading his great hands over the flames as if to warm them, as the others did. He neither ate, nor drank, nor spoke. As Jatsang nodded in the fire's warmth, Sangay saw the *tulpa*'s form grow vague and insubstantial, translucent almost, so that the dim outlines of bushes and rocks showed through his flesh. For a long time Sangay watched and waited, curious to see what would happen when the sorceress slept, but finally he fell asleep himself.

They set out again at dawn, plunging down a series of steep hillsides into lowland jungle. Here the ground was wet and yielding underfoot, the air sharp with the swamp-smell of decay. From either side of the path high walls

of flowering shrubs pressed in upon them.
Like so much else in this strange land, the
colour and scent of the blossoms seemed subtly wrong. Plum-coloured, magenta, mauve,
viridian, livid as bruises against the dark-green,
waxen leaves, they filled the air with a sickly
perfume. Sangay's feet made a squelching
sound as he trod upon the spongy track. His
throat was clogged with the marsh-reek and
the smell of rotting flowers.

Presently, as the ground rose again, they
reached the edge of a forest full of copper-coloured trees. It had a kind of marvellous artifice
about it, like a painted forest in a *manip*'s box.
The bright, metallic leaves were veined with
black, as delicately as silk embroidery, and spot-
ted here and there with verdigris. As the wind
rose, the wood was filled with soft clattering,
clashing sounds like temple-chimes. Truly,
thought Sangay, this was a forest where holy
saints might walk, or gods.

Leaves like thin flakes of copper-foil brushed
against their faces. As they went farther into the
wood, a glimmering red-gold carpet covered
the path. But now the light was fading, and

among the trees were shifting, whispering shadows, dark as fire-blackened bronze.

Sangay could hear the soft clashing of the leaves, the faint sighing of the wind through the branches, and the occasional snap of a twig under Jatsang's feet. And then, gradually, a new and unfamiliar sound crept into the stillness: a slithering, a seething, a rasping, that lifted the hair on the back of his neck.

Something was raising itself up, uncoiling itself with a slow terrible purpose out of the clotted shadows of the wood. Suddenly, all around them, the mountainous shapes of serpents loomed black as charred wood against the bronze gleam of the trees. Their tongues spat flame, venom dripped and hissed from their jaws. Where their breath struck the air a dense bile-green vapour churned and swirled.

Sangay drew his sleeve across his face, an instant too late; a tendril of the green mist, curling down from the upper air, had wrapped itself like a scarf around his head. He felt the sharp sting of it in his nostrils and the roof of his mouth, burning its way down his throat. As his lungs spasmed, he heard the tight, agonized whistling of his breath.

Sangay sank to his knees, choking, retching; his chest was on fire. And then Jatsang was kneeling beside him, pressing to his face a scrap of cloth soaked in an oily liquid smelling pungently of herbs. As he sucked air through the wet cloth, Sangay felt his chest loosen a little, and the terrible burning eased.

Jatsang's hand gripped his arm and he heard her voice low and fierce in his ear. "They are creatures of your mind, Sangay. I cannot help you — you must save yourself. If you have no fear they cannot harm you." With those same words, as softly spoken, had Wanjur once vanquished Sangay's demons, but this time Sangay could take no comfort in them. He was sick with terror, rooted where he crouched. He was aware of nothing in the world but a black glitter of scales, a restless swaying of wedge-shaped heads, a darting of forked tongues, a writhing of mist, a vast, undulating, inescapable movement.

His heart was a hollow drum in his chest, his blood was dust in his veins.

"I cannot . . . " he managed to gasp out. And then huge hands were grasping him by the waist, swinging him high into the air. Tossed unceremoniously across the *tulpa*'s shoulder, Sangay was not so much carried as wafted aloft, a feather suspended on a pillar of cloud. The *tulpa* was tall as a mountain now, but with as little substance as the rank green gases that billowed around them.

Gently, almost tenderly, the *tulpa* set Sangay down. The copper forest lay behind them, a black wall half-hidden in drifting clouds of serpent's breath. Green meadows stretched before them, bright with gentian and summer lilies. In the farthest distance, the sun glittered on ice-crowned peaks.

***

For three days they had been travelling along a windswept ridge. Above lay cold grey slabs of rock; below, a narrow alpine lake skinned over with ice. At these heights there was neither shelter nor wood for a fire. Sangay dozed uneasily, his bones aching from the cold. Curled up in her skin cloak, Jatsang slept undisturbed. Beside her, the *tulpa* snored faintly. In sleep he did not vanish, but grew pale and nebulous, like clotted mist. There was no more human warmth in that great billowy shape than in a bank of summer clouds, but still Sangay took comfort from his presence.

On the third night they came to the end of the ridge and descended into fir woods. Sangay gathered armloads of dead branches for fuel, and broke off some of the lower limbs to make a bed. His spirits lifted, thinking how comfortably he would sleep that night.

At dawn, while Jatsang still slept, he rose and gathered a fresh stack of firewood.

"What are you planning to do with that?" asked Jatsang, mildly curious and half asleep, as she watched him bundle it up with a cord.

"Carry it on my back," said Sangay. "There's high ground ahead, and I mean to be warm for another night at least."

Jatsang made a noise somewhere between a groan and a yak's grunt, indicating her disgust. "It will weigh you down like a stone," she pointed out, "and you have trouble enough to keep up as it is."

"Think how much faster I will walk after a good night's sleep," said Sangay stubbornly.

Jatsang shrugged. "Give it to the *tulpa* to carry, then."

"But he is a knight," said Sangay, shocked.

Jatsang looked at him with amused contempt. "He is a *tulpa*," she said.

But Sangay shook his head. Phantom shape though he might be, the *tulpa* had the true look and bearing of a Hero-Knight. To treat such a being as a mere servant, a bearer of firewood, would be a disrespectful and unseemly act. And so Sangay shouldered his burden himself, though — just as Jatsang had predicted — the weight of it slowed his steps on the steep parts of the path.

As for Jatsang, uphill and downhill were all the same to her, and perversely, it seemed, she had stepped up the pace. For all that he was mountain-born, Sangay found his chest growing tight in the thin air. Finally, as he began to lose ground, Jatsang turned and snarled at him, "In the name of all the vulture-headed ones, Sangay, you try my patience too much. Either throw that wood in the gorge, or let the *tulpa* carry it."

And so he surrendered his burden to the *tulpa*, who gave him a cheerful grin and tossed the bundle onto his shoulder as though it had no weight at all.

Sangay marched on with lightened steps, still thinking about the hot meal and the warm bed he would enjoy that night.

Towards evening they came to a gorge spanned by a narrow, swaying bridge of bamboo poles. The farther side was hidden in mist, and white water raged below. Jatsang stepped out cautiously, with Sangay close behind, setting his feet down slowly and carefully on the ice-slick surface. He stepped off the far side of the bridge with a small sigh of relief, then realized that the *tulpa*, whom he had thought was close behind him, was nowhere to be seen. What could have become of him? Sangay peered anxiously through the mist. Surely this huge, brave warrior was not afraid of heights?

Then, as a gust of wind parted the fog-curtain, Sangay saw the *tulpa*. He was standing in the centre of the bridge, with his back turned to Sangay. He had unfastened the rope on Sangay's precious bundle of firewood, and slowly, deliberately, like a child absorbed in a favourite game, he was dropping the sticks one by one into the river below.

"*Tulpa*," shouted Sangay, in bafflement and helpless rage. Hearing his cry, Jatsang whirled round. The *tulpa* turned too, gazing at Sangay with malicious glee as he tossed the last piece of firewood into the abyss.

* * *

They had been travelling for many days, and as the country grew ever wilder and more strange, so too did the behaviour of the *tulpa*-knight. Where once he had followed them with a dog's docile obedience, now he slunk at their heels like a great stalking cat, so that they were forever watching their backs. At times he fell so far behind they thought they had lost him, and yet in the narrowest places he seemed to take a malign delight in crowding them to the edge. In appearance, too, he had altered. Sangay saw with dismay how lean and scraggy he had become. The great broad face, once so placid and sweet-natured, had a haggard look, and into the eyes there had crept a hint of something sly and manipulative.

"Jatsang," said Sangay, in grief and bewilderment, "what is happening to the *tulpa*?"

Jatsang glanced over her shoulder to make sure their troublesome companion was safely out of earshot. "Alas, it's as my teacher warned me," she replied. "I did not heed him, for I imagined I was too strong, too clever. But as you see, Little Monk, the *tulpa* is no longer my creature. He has become a thing apart from me, possessed of his own will."

"But what will you do, Lady?"

"Do? Why, I suppose I will have to destroy him."

Sangay's heart sank. Do you destroy a faithful guard dog because he digs up your garden or eats your shoes? Sangay would have answered no — but he was not Jatsang.

"Please, Lady," said Sangay, "do not kill the *tulpa*. He acts out of thoughtlessness, like a child — maybe if we are patient, he will mend his ways."

"How long shall I wait?" asked Jatsang. "Shall I wait until he drops *me* over the cliff instead of the firewood? If he is set loose in the world he'll be a danger to anyone who crosses his path."

It was as though the *tulpa* had heard, or sensed, those words, so quietly spoken. When they halted, high up on the mountainside on a rocky ledge, to eat their evening meal, the *tulpa* hovered over them, an irritating and unsettling presence. His expression was wheedling, cajoling, sly as a monkey's. He reached out a hand to grasp the hem of Jatsang's robe; roughly, she slapped it away.

"Where is the tea?" Jatsang wanted to know. She upturned her pouch, shaking out bits of dried-up cheese, crumbs of buckwheat cake, a few grimy grains of rice. Scowling, she peered into its empty depths. "Sangay?" she said accusingly.

"I have not touched your pack," he said. His voice, in his own ears, sounded shrill and defensive; the *tulpa* had set his nerves on edge. Jatsang looked at the *tulpa*, who returned her gaze with cheerful insolence. Mimicking her, he pretended to hold an imaginary pouch, and fumbled through the invisible contents with his great, splay-fingered hands.

"Accursed one," said Jatsang, in a voice so soft that Sangay could barely make out the words, "What have you done with our tea?"

The *tulpa* rose and strolled to the edge of the precipice. Gleefully, he pointed into the yawning gulf below.

An awful silence followed. Sangay held his breath, waiting to see what would happen next. Jatsang's face was white with fury, but all she said to the *tulpa*, in a curiously flat, indifferent voice, was "I am sick of the sight of you, *tulpa*. Go sleep behind those rocks, where we do not have to look at you."

Instead of obeying, the *tulpa* moved deliberately closer to the fire. Jatsang ignored him, and Sangay knew that the decision had been made. From now on, she would simply bide her time. After a while, like a bored child, the *tulpa* began to scoop up handfuls of small stones and toss them into the air. Tiring of that game, he threw one at Jatsang, hard enough to sting, and barely missed her head.

Clearly, the time had come. "Go," said Jatsang to the *tulpa*, her voice low and furious. "You are banished from this world. I have no more need of you."

The *tulpa* got heavily to its feet. What a clumsy, shambling creature it had become, thought Sangay, when once it had been a thing of grace and dignity. Where now was the noble friend, the brave protector who had snatched him from the serpents' jaws? Heartsick and without hope, Sangay offered up one final plea. "Maybe we do not need him now, Lady, but think of the journey that lies ahead. . . ."

"For what will we need him?" Jatsang snapped. "To tramp through the fire, and wreck our belongings, and ruin our firewood, and split our heads with rocks? We can manage well enough without him, Little Monk. This is a demon I have called up, and I will be rid of him."

The *tulpa* stared sullenly at Jatsang, defying her. And then slowly he began to walk towards her — stiff-jointed, swaying, like a wooden temple-image imbued with unholy life.

"Back, back," Jatsang hissed. Her jaw was clenched so hard that all the cords in her neck stood out. She began to curse the *tulpa*, a furious gust of words streaming from her lips. She leaped and whirled, stamping her feet hard on the ground at every turn as though she were crushing the *tulpa*'s head beneath her heels. She hurled more curses, spells of banishment, mystic syllables, exorcisms. All the while the *tulpa* — insolent, unmoved, immovable — went on staring at her with cold, inhuman eyes. Finally, in her fury, Jatsang raised her hands and in a low, terrible voice she spoke a last dreadful incantation. Sangay felt a blast of icy wind howl down across the plateau. So suddenly did it descend, and with such unexpected force, that Sangay was nearly blown off his feet. Staggering to regain his balance and pressing himself against the cliff-face, Sangay saw that the wind had caught the *tulpa* and lifted him up like a great air-filled bladder. Now it was sweeping him irresistibly towards the edge of the precipice. Over he went at last, tossing and swaying like a monstrous kite, drifting and turning in that vast grey gulf of air.

The wind buffeted the *tulpa*, tore at his hair and garments, rasped at him with sand and grit scoured up from the empty mountain-tops. And finally, in its frenzy, it ripped head from shoulders, limbs from body, flesh from bone. Tattered scraps of the *tulpa*, whipped and tossed like prayer-flags, hung for an instant in the icy air; and then they dissipated.

Jatsang sighed, shivered a little, and with the slow stiff movements of exhaustion, turned back to the fire.

"We are rid of him at last," she said. "He will not return."

In her voice there was neither relief nor satisfaction — only a sorrowing acceptance. Moved by comradeship, and his own grief, and a sudden unexpected pity, Sangay crept closer to her side.

"May you be happy," he whispered. "May you be peaceful. May you be free from pain." They were the words he would have spoken to a fellow monk — the only words of comfort he could find.

Jatsang gazed down at him. Her face seemed gentler, younger, in that flickering light. "Tell me, Little Monk," she said, "he *was* a fine *tulpa*, was he not? Better even than the thirty fire-demons . . . "

"Yes," said Sangay, sadly. "Surely better even than those."

Jatsang gave him a wry smile. Then she yawned, and stretched until all her joints cracked, and threw another juniper-branch onto the flames.

THE INCENSE MOUNTAINS

Next morning Sangay and Jatsang reached the northern edge of the plateau, and came down into a green valley filled with groves of sandalwood.

There stretched before them, under a sky of intense, cloudless aquamarine, a lake as calm and luminously blue as a sheet of lapis lazuli. Beyond its white shores rose a line of rocky spires and pinnacles. Rose-red, crimson, topaz, emerald, broken by deep violet shadows, they glowed like jewels in the summer light. Everywhere Sangay recognized the marvellous shapes, the vivid hues, the strange and shining clarity of his dream.

"Look there," said Jatsang, shielding her eyes against the sun's glare. She pointed across the lake to the jewel-coloured peaks. "There are the Incense Mountains, where the sages live. We will ask them to read the writing on your scroll."

Sangay looked at her with faint alarm. These sages, he knew, were powerful *yogis*, initiates into arcane mysteries. In the Dzong one spoke of such men with reverence and awe. Jatsang, off-handed as ever, might have been proposing to ask some passing yak-herd the way to the next village.

"What offerings shall I make?" asked Sangay. "The food is all gone. We have no scarves to present. Shall I give them the zi-stones? Or the sacred dagger?"

Jatsang shook her head impatiently. "Keep those. You may yet have need of them. Come, I will show you."

She led him to the lake's edge, where a white drift of lotus flowers clung to the bank. "There are your offerings," she said.

Kneeling in the warm ooze, Sangay began to gather the delicate cup-shaped blossoms. Jatsang squatted beside him, holding open a large, not very clean silk bag. "Have a care," she admonished. "See if you can manage not to bruise them, or crush them, or step on them, or fall into the lake."

When the bag was full she gave it to Sangay to carry, and they went on, moving northward into the mountains.

Presently they came upon two tall columns of red stone standing like sentinels on either side of the track. Passing through the narrow cleft between, they found themselves encircled by another valley — a secret, sheltered place. Silver streams flowed through it, winding among green fields and water-gardens, and all along its walls, guarding it, stood rows of gigantic rock formations. Like temple-towers, thought Sangay, gazing up at those sheer-sided, graceful shapes. Like towers — or like enchanted cities suspended between earth and sky; for now he saw that their smooth outward faces were honeycombed with caves, and threaded with narrow winding staircases carved into the rock.

The sun was warm on Sangay's back. A soft breeze, soughing through fields of aromatic herbs, filled the air with their heady scent. Thinking of the hard journey that lay behind them, the unknown perils that lay ahead, Sangay breathed a small prayer that Jatsang — who seemed always to act on the whim of the moment — might choose to rest here for a while. But she strode on, as though she had no time to waste, and all Sangay could do was to follow silently behind.

At the far end of the valley the path dissolved into a tumble of red boulders, and they began to climb. On rope ladders and steep, narrow staircases they made their way up the sheer, smooth face of a cliff. Needing both hands free, Sangay fastened the drawstring of the silk bag to his pack and let it billow out behind.

Halfway between the earth and clouds sat the sixteen sages. Their hermitage was a long row of caves set into the cliff's face — no ordinary monks' cells, these, but marvellous jeweled rooms encrusted on roofs and walls with jade, rose-quartz, turquoise, agate, lapis lazuli. Seated lotus-fashion on silk cushions in their robes of embroidered silk, the sages looked serene and changeless as a row of Buddha-figures. Their eyes were the pure piercing blue of mountain lakes, eyes that saw clear through to the soul, and yet in that calm, steady gaze there was as well a childlike and disarming sweetness.

Sangay moved from one jewelled cave-mouth to another, and at the feet of each sage he laid a single lotus-flower. As he completed his task, there arose from the throats of the sixteen sages a wonderful and unearthly sound. In those joined voices Sangay imagined he could hear the voices and sounds of all things in the universe that breathed and moved. It was a music as simple and immediate as the wind's voice among the rocks, or birdsong, as vast as endless space. Like bubbles of pure light the mystic syllables rose, and burst, and vanished. And then silence fell, and Sangay knew that something was demanded of him. Helplessly he turned to Jatsang.

Scowling, she made impatient motions with her hands, as though to urge him forward.

"What must I do?" he whispered in sudden panic. He felt like a raw postulant thrown into the midst of some complex ritual.

Jatsang said, "Do what you came to do, yak-brained one. Give them the scroll."

And with a smile of infinite gentleness, as though he understood and forgave all Sangay's awkwardness, one of the sages held out a frag-ile, parchment-coloured hand. With relief and gratitude Sangay gave up the first of his treasures.

Slowly the old man unrolled the scroll and held it up to the light. In silence he examined the ancient spirit-writing, and at last he spoke.

"Indeed, this is a great treasure you have brought us. This is the writing of the Dakini Yeshe Tsogyal, Princess of Kharchen — she who recorded the teachings of Guru Rimpoche. Are you then a *terton*, a seeker after hidden wisdom?"

Remembering how he had given up the scroll to the bandit-lord to save his own worthless life, Sangay's face flushed with shame.

"Once I dreamed of being such a one," he mumbled. "But no, I am only an unworthy monk who has stumbled by accident on secrets I cannot understand, that were meant for wiser eyes than mine."

Could that be the ghost of a smile flickering at the edges of the old man's mouth? "Such treasures are seldom found by accident," he told Sangay. "It is said that Guru Rimpoche, when he had the Princess Yeshe Tsogyal set down these teachings, predicted the day on which they would be discovered, and the names of those who would one day reveal them to the world. Nothing happens without reason. At this time, in this place, you were destined to find this scroll — as I was meant to read it to you. But — " and now those bright blue eyes, as innocent and curious as a child's, looked straight into Sangay's — "You have not said what made you begin this journey."

Slowly, haltingly, seeking words to describe an experience that remained for him almost beyond description, Sangay related his vision. He spoke of the hidden kingdom beyond the snow-peaks at the world's edge, with its frail, beleaguered king. He spoke of the great dance he had beheld in waking dream; and he told the sages how he hoped, like Kunga Gyaltshen, to return with this True Dance of the Gods to the world of humankind.

Surely now, thought Sangay, they will tell me that I am without virtue, because I am without humility. How could I have imagined myself to be worthy of such deeds?

But there was no hint of censure in the old man's voice as he asked, "Do you know the name of this hidden kingdom, Sangay?"

Sangay shook his head. "I only know that it is a place beautiful beyond imagining — a place where gods must dwell."

"Gods," said the sage, "and kings. It is a country ruled by a great and ancient line of kings. Do you know this prayer, Sangay?"

You, the best of holy teachers, shall be born King of Shambhala
To vanquish the army of the barbarians,
To bring to pass the age of perfection.
You will ride a stone horse with the power of the wind.
Your hand will thrust a spear into the heart of the barbarian king.
Thus will the forces of evil be defeated. . . .

Shambhala . . . how often had Sangay heard that name, in rituals, in prayers — and long before he came to the Dzong — in *manip*'s tales. In a hushed voice he repeated the charmed syllables. Shambhala, the place of refuge, the treasure-house of wisdom. The legendary kingdom beyond the farthest peaks. From Shambhala — so said the prophecies — a king would ride forth with four hundred thousand golden chariots, a million fearless warriors, to vanquish all demons, to drive all evil from the world. And after that last great battle would come a golden age of peace. For a thousand years all the nations of the world would flourish under the wise rule of Shambhala's king.

"But," Sangay said, bewildered, "it cannot be Shambhala that I saw. The King . . ."

"Lies near death, attacked by demons, while barbarian armies hammer at his gates," the sage finished for him. "But you see, Sangay, your vision was a true one. The King is dying. The kingdom is besieged. And the path you must follow, if you would learn the True Dance of the Gods, is the road that leads to Shambhala."

"But what road shall I take? I have no map, no guidebook. . . . "

"How have you found your way this far?"

"At first I wandered blindly, following whatever path presented itself. And after that I followed Jatsang."

As he said this, Sangay looked down in embarrassment. What an ill-judged, haphazard enterprise it seemed, when he had to put it into words.

But to his surprise, the old man simply nodded. "Though your eyes may have been blind,
Sangay, your spirit was not. What you have set
out upon is no ordinary journey that can be
charted on a map. It is a pilgrimage, and a true
pilgrim uses no guidebook. As a cloud drifts
through the summer sky, blown by the wind's
breath from one horizon to another, so a
pilgrim lets himself be guided by the wisdom
that rises from the depths of his spirit. In his
innermost mind he knows his destination,
though it may be hidden from his sight. And
that is what you must go on doing, Sangay.
You must follow whatever path presents itself.
And as for Jatsang . . . " He turned his head
and for an instant his eyes and the eyes of the
sorceress met. In that brief glance it seemed
that the two of them shared some unspoken
knowledge. "And as for Jatsang," he said, "I
think she has walked this way before."

"And the scroll?" Sangay reminded him.
"Will you read me what the spirit-writing says?"

The parchment rustled softly in the sage's
hand. "Listen, then, to the words of the Precious Guru." His voice — reedy as *gyaling* music
— rose and fell in the cadences of prayer.

"Have no doubt about this: that all experiences, all peaceful and wrathful forms are the natural manifestations of your mind. All sounds are your own sounds. All lights are your own lights. When you remain unharmed by suffering and difficulties, that is the sign of understanding appearances to be illusion."

Sangay waited. Was that all? Had the old man finished? Were these the words of wisdom that would guide him safely to his journey's end? His throat ached with disappointment. "Yes," he said. "This I know. This I have been taught. This I understand."

Like blue ice, like dagger-blades, those pale eyes pierced him to the soul. "You know," the old man said. "You have been taught. You understand. But Sangay, do you believe?"

And Sangay stood silent and ashamed, for what was being asked of him was absolute, unhesitating truth. And he found, to his dismay, that he could not answer.

Presently the sage said, "As there is a reason for all things, there is a reason for your journey. But what that reason is, you must discover for yourself. On your way you will encounter many dangers, many difficulties. Demons will

confront you, and savage beasts, and all the
terrible forces of nature. Haunted forests, seas
and deserts, raging torrents will bar your
way. . . . Yet if you are to reach your destination,
you must not let your courage fail you. There
is more written upon the scroll. Will you hear
it, Sangay?"

Wretchedly, Sangay nodded.

"These too are the words of the Precious
Guru. They have been revealed to you, unworthy as you may imagine yourself to be — not for
your benefit, Sangay, but for the benefit of all
sentient beings."

He unrolled the scroll still farther. The
other sages leaned forward on their silken
cushions, their faces grave and attentive,
their eyes serene.

"In whatever direction you travel, you must
seek protection from these terrors in the bless-
ings of the Three Jewels, the Three Precious
Things: you must have faith in the Buddha, in
the wisdom of his teachings, and in the companionship of those who have found the True
Path. If you do these things, with true faith and
compassion, then you will be immune to the
terrors of the lower realms. You will be harmed

neither by humans, nor by demons nor malicious spirits, nor by any of the obstacles in this life."

Sangay watched the old man's hands as with practised movements they furled up the scroll and carefully tied the tapes.

"We will keep it safe for you," the sage said gently. "It will be waiting for you, when you return."

Sangay made his farewells and with a troubled spirit he turned away. Over and over, like a mantra, his own words echoed in his mind: "I have been taught. I know. I understand." And always, at the end, the sage's question, still unanswered: "Do I believe?"

THE DESERT OF BLACK GLASS

All day they had been trudging across a flat plain broken by scattered heaps of stones. From time to time there were mudflats, cracked in the dry heat and then baked as stiff as tiles, and fields of ridged black stone, like waves petrified to a glassy hardness.

Everything — ground, sky, rocks — shimmered with heat. The air had that charged, heavy feeling that comes before a storm. There was no sun, only a faint red glow behind churning masses of black cloud.

"How much farther?" gasped Sangay, as they made their way across a sunken field of black glass, covered with a layer of dust the colour of dried blood.

"How much farther to where?" asked Jatsang sourly.

"To *anywhere*," said Sangay, gazing across that dismal and seemingly endless plain.

Jatsang shrugged. Just then a fiery gust of wind swept down upon them, snatching away their breath and sending columns of red dust spinning into the air. Seconds later a great sheet of blue flame crackled across the sky, followed on the instant by an earth-shaking thunder-clap.

The storm broke all around them. The air shuddered and groaned; there was a rumbling and crashing of monstrous kettle-drums; forked serpent-tongues of blue and violet flame drenched the plain in ghastly light. And then, above the crazy howling of the wind, Sangay heard other sounds: a high, demonic shrieking, a wild beating of wings. Dropping out of the livid sky, shaping themselves from empty air as though the storm had given them birth, came hundreds of huge black birds. Sangay glimpsed, in an instant of heart-chilling terror, their crimson eyes, their rapacious beaks, their

talons like curved knives outstretched for the
kill, and then he flung himself headlong to the
ground. In his nostrils was the sulphur stench
of the storm, the dry, acrid smell of the red dust,
whipped by the wind into pillars of flame, and
the carrion reek that blew over him with every
flap of those gigantic wings. There was no shelter anywhere, nowhere that he could run.

"They are not real," he told himself. "They
are not real." Frantically he muttered those
four words again and again, making a mantra
of them. "All sounds are my own sounds. All
lights are my own lights. They are not real, they
cannot harm me."

Black wings flapped all around him. He put
his hands against his ears to muffle the unearthly shrieking, the beating of wings that was
louder and more terrifying than the thunder in
the heavens. Wingtips brushed against his face.
Thick and hot and sickening, the corpse-smell
filled his lungs. Any moment, he thought, those
beaks and claws would rend his flesh.

His lips moved — endlessly, desperately
chanting the words of the Guru. They were all
the weapons he had against these creatures out
of nightmare.

In the middle of his terror and confusion, he felt fingers brushing against his wrist. And then someone gripped his hand — not in fear, but in calm reassurance. The hand felt cool and dry and immensely comforting against his feverish skin.

"Jatsang," he whispered; and back came the soft reply, as much sensed as heard: "I am here. Have courage."

She was so close now that he could feel her breath against his cheek. She said, "If you would save yourself, you must have faith, Sangay. You must believe. These things are not real. They are magic; they are illusion; they are the substance of dreams; they are the reflection of the moon in water. "

The earth rocked beneath him; the sky burned. All around him was the howling of the wind, the blue unearthly light, the enormous thundering of wings. Everything was shifting, changing — the very earth to which he clung was falling away beneath him, and for a dreadful instant he glimpsed above, below, on every side, the endless blackness of the void.

Thin and faint, as from a very long way off, he heard Jatsang's voice. "Illusion, Sangay. All is illusion. Remember the *tulpa.*"

She had made a phantom, a thing of magic, and she had let it become real. It had nearly destroyed her. All this — the birds, the storm, the pillars of dust, the earth's trembling — all these were dreams, and if he forgot they were dreams, they had the power to destroy him.

With a terrible effort of will Sangay raised his head and looked around him. Black wings battered the air, restlessly circling.

Slowly, deliberately, he stood up. He took many slow deep breaths, filling his body and his mind with lightness, stillness, the calm that comes with absolute repose. All that he had learned in his long months of meditation served him now.

"What is there to fear?" he asked himself, shouting out the question as the wings swooped closer. "I have imagined these birds as eagles. So too can I imagine them as anything I please."

They were all a part of the dance, the pattern of things, the Great Mandala, and he was the dance-maker, the one who stood apart and saw the pattern. As he stared steadfastly at the birds he watched the great talons retract, the fierce beaks dwindle, the wings and the bodies shrink, shape-shift. The necks grew slender and graceful, the dull black feathers took on brilliant rainbow hues of blue and purple-green and chestnut-red. Long, elegant tail feathers sprouted. He imagined them pheasants, and pheasants they became.

Now, gathering strength and confidence, he quieted the wind, rolled back the thunderheads, brought light and colour into the sky, transformed the leaping pillars of flame into sunlit fountains, carpeted the black, glassy plain with grass and flowers.

Where once he had known, had understood, now at last he believed; and in believing, he had transformed the world.

THE DEMONS IN THE WOOD

Their path, next morning, led them into the depths of an ancient forest of oak and pine. The trunks of the trees were blotched with lichen and festooned with creeping vines, their branches forming a dark roof overhead. The air smelled of wet earth and decay. The track, hedged in by bramble thickets and tall stands of bamboo, twisted and turned and in places almost disappeared. In the distance they could hear a steady rushing sound, like a waterfall or a strong wind.

"It must be the voice of the River Sita," Jatsang remarked. "They say that its waters are like the wind that blows when the world ends."

Waiting impatiently for Sangay to climb over a deadfall, she added, "They say, also, that whoever is touched by the waters of the Sita is turned to stone."

"Then how shall we cross such a river?" Sangay asked in dismay.

Jatsang lifted a nonchalant shoulder. "Why ask me?" that shrug might have said. Or "Such is fate." Or possibly, "What is one more obstacle in our way?"

As they went farther into the forest, the grey-green murk deepened. Shadows dripped from the branches, puddled at their feet. Red eyes peered from the undergrowth. From a giant clump of bamboo came a sound of growling and snarling, and then a series of not quite human grunts. Worse yet was an ominous cracking, splintering noise like bones being crunched. Once Sangay had overheard a village woman say, "My flesh crawled." Now he understood what she had meant.

Meanwhile, incessant and inescapable, above them and all around them, was the roar of the River Sita.

"Go carefully," warned Jatsang. "Never step from the straight path, and never look behind you."

The last of the light faded. Night swept down upon them. Crouched under the roots of a fallen oak they tried to make a fire, but each time they coaxed a small flame into life it sputtered and smoked and went out.

Something large crashed through the underbrush. Sangay's hair rose on his neck. "The wood is too damp," he said. "It will never burn. Can't you use your magic?"

"Magic calls to magic," Jatsang replied. "I fear what we may attract."

The darkness crowded in on Sangay, smothering and oppressive as a pillow over his face. With a patience borne of desperation, he managed to produce a little, smouldering fire. But now, in its uncertain light, he saw what the darkness had mercifully concealed.

In a circle around their makeshift camp were a dozen lurching figures — nightmare creatures, half-beast, half-human, shambling on two legs like dancing bears. Their faces were obscured by manes of black, matted, bloodstained hair.

Sangay shrank back against Jatsang. "What are they?" he whispered, throat clotted with fear. "Are they real or only illusions?"

"All things are illusion," Jatsang reminded him. "Yet in this place, at this moment, they are real enough. They are the Night-Travellers, the Eaters of Flesh. They are messengers from the Dark Realms, from the Lord of Death."

"What do they want from us?"

"Quite clearly," said Jatsang, "they want to eat us."

Sangay swallowed hard. Jatsang did not make jokes.

"They are afraid of fire," Jatsang said. "But if the fire goes out . . . "

The fire chose that moment to hiss, and flicker, and subside to a hesitant wisp of flame.

"Then better to die at once," Sangay decided, "than to sit here and wait to be eaten. I have my bow, you have your knives. . . . "

"No material weapon can harm these creatures," Jatsang said. " They feed on your fear. If you are afraid, they will devour you. You must make a Circle of Protection."

"How am I to do that?"

"First you must enter the meditative state."

Sangay stared at her. How could he meditate, when his pulse raced with terror, when his heart thumped like a kettle-drum in his throat? When at any instant the fire might go out, and monsters waited to devour him?

All the same, he sat down in the lotus position, legs folded, back erect. He emptied his lungs of air, then breathed in deeply, making his chest the shape of an earthen pot. In, out, in, out. As he breathed, the hammering of his heart slowed and he felt his mind grow calmer.

Jatsang sat facing him, knee to knee, eye to eye. She began to guide him, as serenely, as confidently, as she had led him over the high passes.

"Each time you breathe out, imagine that innumerable rays of light are emanating from every pore of your body, and filling the whole world. Now see their colours — they are blue for ether, green for air, red for fire, white for water, yellow for earth. And when you breathe in, these rays are filling every cell of your body. Seven times you must do this."

Sangay breathed in, breathed out. The light, the colours, the radiance, flowed out into the universe, and into the deepest places of his being. His mind, and the universe, was filled with the sacred syllable HUM.

He felt Jatsang's hands resting lightly on his shoulders. A warmth passed through them, into his flesh. "Now imagine" — and somehow her words were no longer sounds in his ears, but images in his head — "that each one of those rays of light is changed into a fierce and angry goddess. Each goddess holds her left hand against her heart, and with her right hand she flourishes above her head a knife with a curving blade. Her face, which is of five colours, is menacing and terrible. And every pore of your body is inhabited by a wrathful goddess, surrounding you and protecting you like a suit of chain mail."

Hours might have passed, or days, or moments. Sangay had entered a place where there was no passage of time, no difference between dreams and waking. No difference between Jatsang's thoughts and his. As the energies of their bodies were linked by the light pressure of Jatsang's hands, so also were their minds joined. He saw the world through Jatsang's inward eye, as Jatsang saw it — the stuff of which dreams are shaped. The only real things in the universe were the countless millions of fierce and wrathful guardian spirits, each one no larger than a sesamum seed, that inhabited his being. What teeth, what claws could penetrate such armour? He felt himself invincible.

Then, as though from a long way off, outside of himself, he heard Jatsang's voice.

"Open your eyes, Sangay. Return to the world."

He stirred, roused, and looked around him. Beyond the smoking embers of the fire he saw only a black wall of pines rising out of mist and shadow. The night-demons were gone.

All his muscles felt slack, relaxed. He was drained of everything but a deep calm, and an immense relief.

"They were drawn by your fear," Jatsang said. "When you lost your terror, they vanished into the night."

CROSSING THE RIVER SITA

Sangay and Jatsang stepped from the shadows at the forest's edge into brilliant light. Before them was a broad river-shore of white sand and glittering pebbles, with green slopes rising above. Confined by its steep banks, the Sita raged and bellowed like a furious caged beast. On the near bank stood a row of stone figures, so cleverly carved that from a distance one might imagine they lived and breathed. Monks and nuns, abbots and sages in embroidered robes, sorcerers in five-pointed hats, all straggled along the shore like a procession of lost pilgrims, frozen in time.

Jatsang laid a warning hand on Sangay's arm. He saw her lips move; the words were lost in the roar of the water. She beckoned and he followed her.

Some distance upstream was a grassy bluff which overlooked the river. Here, out of reach of the deadly spray, they crouched and gazed down.

Just under the churning surface they could see slender, darting shapes. From neck to tail these creatures were scaled and sinuous, fish-like, but their heads were the heads of birds and animals: parrots, monkeys, panthers, tigers, sheep. Sangay watched one glide to the surface, trailing a dark net of hair. For the space of a held breath its eyes met Sangay's. The smooth brow, the tender mouth, the pale and slanting cheeks, belonged to the face of a young girl.

They were things of grace and beauty, these strange fish that danced in the waters of the Sita, and the sight of them filled Sangay's soul with horror.

He turned to Jatsang. "How can we cross such a torrent? Must every test be harder than the last? See," he said, pointing downstream to where the stone figures marched along the bank. "Look how many others have tried and failed. Is there no other road we can take?"

"No road that leads to Shambhala, Sangay. If you turn aside now, you will never find your way back to the true path. What you must do is to seek the help of the King of Fish. But first, you must make him an offering."

Sangay had never made an offering to a fish. He glanced towards Jatsang, hoping for advice, but she had settled herself comfortably under a tree and was opening the flask of *arra*. Go look for yourself, her shrug said.

A tangle of vines grew along the slope behind them. Sangay searched under the leaves, found clusters of small, round, honey-coloured fruit. He snatched up as many as he could carry, stuffed them into his robe, and trudged back to the river-bank.

"Now you must say a mantra," Jatsang told him. Obediently he folded himself into the lotus position. "*Om mani padme hum,*" he chanted, the O vibrating up from the depths of his belly, the M like a sighing of wind upon his lips.

Far below him something splashed and rippled. Cautiously Sangay peered over the edge

of the bluff. A short distance downstream,
where an arm of the river coiled among roots
and logs through a reedy backwater, an
astonishing creature circled. From gill to tail-
fin his body was a glittering curve of silver and
gold and purple scales. But the dripping head
that he lifted out of the water was the head of
a great blue sheep.

"May you be happy, fish," said Sangay politely, moving closer. "May you be peaceful.
May you be free from suffering." And he
dropped the golden fruits over the edge of the
cliff into the water. At once the King of Fish
snatched them up and devoured them.

Then Sangay said, "Oh King of Fish, I am
going to Shambhala for the benefit and happiness of all sentient beings."

"And in what way does this concern me?"
asked the King of Fish, as he swallowed the last
of the fruit. Irritably he tossed his blue-grey
sheep's head with its stout backward-sweeping
horns. A trickle of golden juice ran down from
his jaws.

"I want you to help me cross this river,"
Sangay said.

"Then why don't you jump in?" asked the King of Fish. "Are you afraid I will pierce you on my horns? Or . . . " and now his expression grew sly, "maybe you are unable to swim?"

"No one can swim in these waters," replied Sangay. "One touch will freeze my blood and turn my flesh to stone."

"So you say," mused the King of Fish. "I have noticed, of late, that the temperature was a little cool for comfort. That fruit, on the other hand, was excellent. Did you say there was more?"

Sangay turned uncertainly to Jatsang. "He is a greedy old goat," she remarked. "Still, you'd better do as he asks."

Sangay raced up the hillside and gathered armloads of fruit. He hurled them into the water, and one by one the King of Fish snatched them up.

"Now then," said the fish, picking up the thread of the conversation where he had left off, "your tall companion there — I observe that she is wearing a magician's hat. The cold is no matter to one who is trained in the sorcerer's arts. You must ask her to carry you across on her back."

Jatsang stepped closer, scowling. "Clearly," she said, "this fish will not listen to reason. He is an unenlightened fish, full of covetousness, mistaken beliefs and ill will. He possesses neither wisdom, nor gentleness, nor compassion."

"All this may be true," said Sangay, "but how does it alter the situation?"

"Since we cannot argue with him," said Jatsang, "let us see if we can frighten him. Look there — " and she pointed upstream. There, where the river surged to the west through a gorge, rose a high copper-coloured cliff pockmarked with thousands of caves.

"In the nearest one of those caves," said Jatsang, "there is said to live a demoness. Her name is Flashing Lightning. You must ask for her help."

At the mouth of the cave Sangay placed offerings of flowers and fruit, and chanted mantras, and drew the she-demon's imagined image in the sand.

After a while he heard a shrill scraping, like the sound of fingernails on rocks, and a good deal of grunting and threshing, as though a very large creature was moving about in a small space. Black smoke billowed suddenly from the cave mouth; there was a smell of burning. And then Sangay's stomach closed on itself like a fist.

She had three heads, one pale as milk, one red as blood, the third blue-black, like a thunder-cloud. In each of those heads, three eyes glared, wide-open and furious, under quivering black brows. The three mouths were crowded with protruding teeth, long and yellow-grey and glistening, the top ones jutting downward so that they almost bit into her lower lip. From between those teeth came shrill whistling sounds. Her hair stood out all around her heads and glowed with its own fierce light, so each head seemed haloed with fire.

Now the shoulders were emerging, and the massive chest, garlanded with a necklace of black snakes, and then six arms, each one the size of a tree-trunk. The demoness used her elbows and knees to pull herself the rest of the way through, for in each of her six hands was an object: a red conch-shell, a noose of serpent fangs, a three-pronged spear, a club, a battle-axe, a cup fashioned from a human skull. And then she was on her feet, those dreadful heads glowering down on Sangay from three times his height, and he bit down on his lip and dug his nails into his palms to still his trembling.

"What else have you got for me?" asked Flashing Lightning.

Sangay stared at her, too frightened to speak.

What else could he give her? He fumbled in his robe for the deerskin bag. She could not have the *phurba*. And not the scroll — she would only set it alight. The rice, tea, and the buckwheat flour were nearly gone. And then he remembered the zi-stones.

Since the demoness's hands were occupied, he scattered the stones at her feet.

"What is your wish?" asked the demoness. Her voice was like the rumbling of temple-drums — the roar of an avalanche down mountain steeps — like thunder.

"I wish to cross the River Sita," Sangay said. His voice shook, but he managed to get the words out.

"Then I suggest you do so. Why are you troubling me about it?"

"Because one touch of its waters turns human flesh to stone."

The she-demon pondered this for a moment.

"Why do you not ask the King of Fish to help you? He is a powerful *yogi*."

"We have asked the King of Fish. He will not listen to our pleas."

"He will listen to mine," said Flashing Lightning. Sangay felt the ground shake as she strode down the grassy slopes to the river bank.

At the edge of the water she lowered herself into the lotus position. "Fish," she bellowed, over the crash and roar of the water.

The King of Fish swam lazily into view.

"Fish," said the demoness, "you will help these pilgrims across the river."

"And if I refuse?"

"Then," said Flashing Lightning, "I will blow my conch-shell, to summon you up on this river-bank. I will catch your horns in my noose of serpents-fangs, and I will pin you to the ground with my three-pronged spear. I will crack your thick skull with my club, and with my battle axe I'll chop off your head. And then I will use my skull-cup to drink your blood."

And with that she rose to her full height, her six arms brandishing these awful objects high above her head, her hair flying out in the wind like flames. She lifted the red conch-shell to her mouth, and began to blow. The sound of the conch was louder, deeper, more thunderous even than the river's roar. It was the sound of all the storms of the world unleashed together, the sound of mountains toppling. The King of Fish swam frantically in circles. His eyes bulged; he choked and flailed. Louder and louder the conch roared. Slowly the great fish slid out of the water — drawn up and up as though a hook impaled him. Gasping and squirming, he came to rest on a ledge of hard stones halfway up the bank.

The demoness bore down upon him, brandishing a weapon in every hand.

"Have pity on me," the fish pleaded.

"If you would be shown compassion, you must show some yourself," said the demoness. "Tell these travellers how they may cross the River Sita."

The fish gasped again, and beat his tail against the rocks. "If they were not such poor fools of humans, they would know. They must turn the power of the river against itself."

"And how are they to do that? Speak, fish, while there is still life in your body." She waved the spear for emphasis.

"They must summon the river out of its banks, and hurl it back upon itself," the fish said.

Sangay looked at Jatsang. "Is it a trick?"

She shrugged. "It may be. But if we are to go on, we must chance it. Will you help me, Sangay?" He nodded.

"Remember," she said, "If you lose heart . . . if you cease for so much as an instant to believe, then we are lost."

They stood shoulder to shoulder on the bank, and with the joined force of their minds, their souls, their wills, they drew up those raging waters, as the wind draws up the desert sands. The waters rose in a churning wall, curling high above their heads, above the tops of the tallest trees. And there it hung against the sky, a glittering, sun-spangled, foam-crested curtain.

In some corner of his mind Sangay felt Jatsang's presence. Wordlessly she calmed him, steadied him. Had either of them wavered for a single instant, had they let their concentration slip for a heart-beat's space, that whole colossal wall would have crashed down upon them.

Then, when he thought that instant must go on forever, he felt Jatsang's urgent thought. "Now, Sangay." And with every ounce of strength and determination that remained to him, he forced the wall of waters back and back. It rippled and swayed, its edges tearing, and at last, with a thunderous roar, it collapsed in on itself.

Where there had been a raging river there now lay, between the high banks, a shining road of solid ice.

Jatsang seized Sangay's arm, dragged him down the slope; and slipping a little in their soft boots, they raced across the slick white surface, as easily as one crosses a bamboo bridge. The instant their feet touched the opposite bank, they heard a seething and cracking, as the ice shattered into pieces, and the river, more furious than ever, burst up like molten lava from below. Looking back, Sangay saw that the demoness had already vanished; and so had the King of Fish.

The Wall
at the World's End

North from the River Sita, green meadows and orchards sloped away towards forested hills. From a village close by came the sound of temple bells, the hum and clatter of a market-place. The wind smelled of spices, and flowers, and roasting meat. Sangay's mouth watered and his belly growled. But Jatsang strode on without slackening her pace. Glancing wistfully over his shoulder, Sangay followed her away from the village, across a field of saffron cro-cuses and into the dappled shade of a birch grove.

As they walked through the grove Sangay could hear soft laughter, like the patter of rain, like bark rustling. Half-hidden among the silvery branches, dark leaf-shaped eyes watched him. A chorus of voices, high and sweet as singing birds, called out: "Come, rest for a while. The road is long. Why hurry?"

With all his heart Sangay yearned to set down his burdens. The voices promised comfort, respite. Slyly, they hinted at delight. But Jatsang sensed at once that his resolve was weakening. Wheeling round, she glowered at him with the face of a wrathful demoness.

"If you are wise you'll stop your ears," she said. "Stray from the path for so much as an hour, and be sure you will never find your way again."

And then, abruptly as the landscape of a dream changes, the woods and meadows were behind them, and they were following a maze of narrow paths through winter mountains. Once again they had entered a desolate world of stone and mist and cold grey light. Surely, thought Sangay, shivering as the wind came up and sky darkened, there will never be an end to this journey. Exhaustion seized him, and a black despair. His steps slowed; he walked as though he carried a dragging weight upon his back.

One evening near dark they floundered their way to the head of a snow-choked valley. As the light faded, thick dirty-grey clouds settled over the crags and precipices, and more snow began to fall. They could go no farther, and they spent the night huddled together, sheltering under a cliff.

By morning the weather had cleared and Sangay woke to patchy sunshine. He left Jatsang still sleeping and went out to see where their path led.

And found that there was no more path.

What last night had been hidden by blowing snow and cloud-bank now loomed inescapably before him. Across a wide, flat snowfield rose a rampart of black ice-streaked stone, as sheer and slick as glass. To east and west it curved away into immeasurable distance, its summits vanishing in the mist.

He had come, at last, to the wall at the world's end, the great ring of snow mountains that surround Shambhala.

Sangay had always known that the wall was there — and yet somehow he had not let himself believe in its existence. Now, at last, he was made to see the sheer wrongheaded hopelessness of his journey.

And so with a hollow aching in his chest he turned to Jatsang — turned to her for aid, for strength, for reassurance.

"What am I to do now?" he asked her. "I have battled monsters and cannibal demons. I have crossed the deserts of black sand and the deadly waters of the Sita. Is this fair, that now I should be defeated by a barrier only an eagle could cross?"

But Jatsang offered him nothing — neither help nor comfort. Her black eyes were shuttered and remote, her face without expression. When he spoke her name she simply stared at him, as one might stare at a stranger on the road. It was as though at this moment of his greatest need she had chosen to abandon him. And because Sangay was not such a fool as to hate the mountain, with all the passion of his despair he turned his anger upon Jatsang.

Furiously he cried, "Why will you not answer me, Jatsang? What shall I do? Shall I travel round the mountain, seeking a way over the heights? In my lifetime, I could not hope to finish such a journey. Or shall I imagine this mountain out of existence? Transform it into a wall of mist and air? Surely the most powerful *yogi* in the world is not equal to the task."

Jatsang shrugged. "So you say. If that is what you believe, then it must be true. Only remember, you chose this road, Sangay, and from here on, you must travel it alone. I have given you what skills I could. Now you must use them."

"Look at that mountain, Jatsang — that is no illusion. It exists. It is real. I cannot think it away."

"Maybe not," said Jatsang. She lounged against a boulder, idly scratching the back of her calf with a filthy toe.

His throat was tight with anger. "What then? Would you have me grow wings, and fly?"

Jatsang leaned back and stared heavenward, as though considering his chances. And at that moment Sangay saw Wanjur's cheerful face, as they crouched together in a cold monastery passageway. Once again he heard Wanjur's voice: "When you are faced with three completely impossible tasks, the least impossible is the one you must choose." How young

Sangay had been then, and how ignorant. In those days no task had seemed impossible.

And then he remembered another time, another place: a cave, darkness, an old man's voice: "The kite cannot choose of itself to soar free into the upper air, to go where the wind takes it. As long as a hand holds the string, it is tied to earth."

I am the kite, thought Sangay, and I am the string, and I am the hand that holds the string.

He settled himself lotus-fashion on the icy ground, his face turned to the north. With long slow breaths he breathed out his anger and resentment, breathed in the knowledge that in this world there is nothing that is truly impossible.

He thought of how far he had come, how many challenges he had met, how many victories he had won. He thought of the old man in the mountain lake, so lightly bound by the laws of this world that iron chains must hold him to the earth.

And then, with a surge of relief and gratitude, he heard Jatsang's voice guiding him, as her hand on his shoulder had guided him over the high, treacherous mountain paths. "Feel the fire, Sangay. Feel the fire that is like the light that burns on the southern edge of the universe. Your mind is a dark wood, Sangay — a tangled, shadowy thicket. Let the fire burn within you. Let it burn away your doubts, your fears, all the confusion that dwells within you."

He filled his head with a single syllable, "HUM", let it grow and grow until there was room for nothing else — neither doubts, nor terror, nor confusion. He felt it, then — a slow warmth rising through him, through his legs, thighs, trunk, chest, throat. It reached his head, and something softened, melted, burst apart into silver drops like a moon exploding into particles of light. Through every vein, every channel of his body the silver flowed. He was lighter than water, lighter than air. He was a cloud, a feather, a leaf upon the wind. And all around him, suddenly, he heard the rushing of wings. There was laughter, and the fragrance of roses, and strong, slender arms lifted him up and up into the diamond-glittering air. The wind blew past his face. He looked down, and saw far below, as though through an eagle's eyes, the mist-wrapped peaks and crags and pinnacles, the bottomless black gorges.

He was a leaf, a scrap of cloud. All around he could hear the tinkling of golden ankle-bells and the unearthly laughter of the Cloud-spirits.

The wind swept down and blew away the mist, and he saw Shambhala, the land beyond the world's end, spread out before him like a great mandala. There were the eight outer kingdoms, each set within its petal-shaped ring of mountains, exactly as in the prophecies, the sacred writings, the *manips'* tales. And there in the innermost kingdom was the capital, Kalapa, the jewel at the heart of the lotus, guarded by its ring of snow-white peaks.

And then Sangay descended, as lightly as a kite floating downward on a draft of wind. The earth drifted slowly up to meet him.

THE WASTELAND

Was this is a cruel joke the gods had played on him? Where were the emerald meadows of Shambhala, the flowering woods, the golden-roofed pagodas? It was as though a curse had fallen over the land. Nothing seemed to grow here now but spiny grey carpets of buckthorn, a few dry tamarisk clumps, some withered stalks of thyme. Northward and westward, parched, dun-coloured grasslands faded into a yellowish mist. To the east was a grey expanse of mud-flats stretching away to the jagged black horizon. The sun was low in the sky and a harsh wind blew, carrying with it a scattering of hail. There was no sign of human habitation, no sound but the sighing of the wind through bare branches and shrivelled grass.

Never had Sangay felt so alone or so dis-
heartened. But there was no turning back, no
choice but to follow the bleak path that lay
before him.

Presently he came to a place where a forest
had once stood. All that remained now was an
expanse of hacked-off stumps. Further on was
a still more dismal region of swamps and salt-
marshes, ringed by black, skeletal trees. Hours
later he could still smell the rank, sour odour
of that blighted earth.

Beyond the dead forest the ground was broken into a series of low ridges and valleys. There
was a smell of woodsmoke on the wind, and
now, as the light faded, he could see small
scattered fires blooming along the hillsides.

Then the silence was broken by hoofbeats
on the hard, dry ground. Black against the
bruised purple of the sunset, five horsemen
rode over the crest of a hill. There was no hope
of escape, and nowhere to hide. An instant later
Sangay was hemmed in by a circle of spear-
points.

Five pairs of cold, iron-grey eyes peered
down at him. No one spoke. There was only the
heavy breath of the ponies, the rustling of the

grass, the faint clicking of a wolf's-tooth necklace as one of the horsemen leaned forward to
scrutinize Sangay more closely.

The horseman's expression was hostile. For
his own part, Sangay felt a curious sense of
detachment. He was well aware that his fate
turned on a shrug, a grunt, a casual spear-
thrust, but he was too tired and dispirited to be
truly afraid. And so he waited, gazing at the
horsemen with a kind of dull resignation.

They were big men, powerfully built, and
taller even than Jatsang. In their leather trousers and padded leather coats, their scaled armour and leopard-skin cloaks, they looked like
giants. There were beads and feathers and bits
of metal woven into their plaited hair and the
bright blonde thickets of their beards. Their
lean, shaggy-coated ponies were as barbarically
outfitted, in antlered masks of leather and coloured felt.

One man, older than the rest, seemed to be
in command. His coat was made of embroidered silk; his polished armour glinted like
lizard's scales under a great cloak of black fur,
worn skin-side out; a bronze torque glimmered

at his throat. Crouched blind-folded across his saddle was a small black hunting leopard.

The man said something in a language which sounded to Sangay as though he had a fishbone stuck in his throat. One of the others laughed. And then the leopard's owner snatched the blindfold from the animal's eyes, and made a kind of clucking sound with his tongue against his teeth.

The leopard sprang down from the saddle and began to creep on its belly towards Sangay, its jaw-muscles bunched, the long sleek muscles of its flanks rippling under its black shaggy coat.

Sangay thought, I do not wish to die now, after having survived so much. But this was no beast of the imagination, to be subdued by mind-magic.

And this time there were no monks to protect him, no Jatsang to leap, weapon in hand, to his defence.

Weapon in hand . . . with that thought, he dropped his hand to his belt and slid the dragon-handled dagger from its sheath.

Almost at once he felt the knife writhing, twisting in his grasp. It was alive. It was a force apart from himself, beyond his control. He opened his fingers, as though to let the knife fall. But it did not fall. Shimmering with a silvery light in the grey air, possessed by its own mysterious power, it rose, hovered, danced.

In that coiled, taut instant before the leopard sprang, one of the horses reared back in terror, its fore-hooves lashing out. The leopard shivered and whimpered, and like a cowed dog sank belly to the ground. Then, mewling plaintively, it turned tail and went slinking back to its master.

The other men stared uneasily at one another, and then at Sangay. Sangay could guess what they were thinking: "See, the beasts know the smell of magic. Surely this is a sorcerer, a shaman in disguise. Better let him go."

But their leader was not so easily impressed. He snarled an order over his shoulder, and wrenching his sword from his belt, leaned forward.

With the return of Sangay's fear came anger. Anger at these men for barring his path when he had already endured so much. Anger at himself, for being afraid. And above all, anger at the devastation they had visited upon this land.

As blood congeals, as air becomes cloud, water becomes snow, snow hardens into ice, so did Sangay give shape and substance to his rage. He had no skill, as Jatsang did, for fashioning fire-demons and warrior-knights. These were malformed, misshapen things, these creatures fashioned from his anger and despair, clumsy as sketches a child makes with a charred piece of wood. They were grey as storm-clouds, thin and tattered and nebulous as mist. As they swayed and flapped behind him, their ragged wings made a faint clicking and clattering, like the rattle of fleshless bones.

The leopard snarled in terror; the horses reared and plunged. Their riders muttered prayers to their own gods as they fought to quiet their beasts. Sangay, under cover of grey, flapping, tattered ghost-wings, scrambled into the shadow of some rocks on the far side of the ridge.

The Lotus-Petalled Land

He heard hoofbeats receding beyond another hill; then there was only the wind's howling, and once or twice a rumble of thunder over the far peaks. All that night he huddled in the lee of the rocks, dozing for a while, waking, listening, dozing again.

In the morning he stumbled upon the ruins of a paved road, wide enough for four horses abreast. Once it must have been a great processional way, leading northward towards Kalapa. Once cavalcades of princes, courtiers, warrior-monks and priests had clattered over these grey stones. Banners and scarlet cloaks and silk umbrellas had swirled, trumpets had blared,

drums had thudded. Now the road was half
hidden in rank growth, weeds thrusting up
between the cracked and loosened cobbles.
Picking his way carefully, Sangay followed it. To
the north, where the road vanished into pearly
haze, Shambhala's innermost mountains
floated like white towers on a lake of mist.

The road led through a huddle of dark
crags, then down into a bleak, treeless valley.
He walked all day along the ruined road, and
finally, at sundown, crested the ridge on the
other side. He could see below him a narrow
strip of glacial moraine, and immediately beyond, the steep southern flanks of Kalapa's
guardian peaks.

From a distance these peaks had looked
milk white, like chalk, or marble. Now, at close
range, he realized that they were not rock at all,
but solid ice. Transparent as glass, they had no
colour of their own but captured instead all the
colours of the sunset, shimmering with soft
reflected tints of rose and gold and amethyst.
Here at last was the final barrier, the gateway to
the Sacred City, but for all that he could reach
it, he might have been standing on the far side
of the world.

All along that boulder-strewn strip of
ground an army was encamped. Fires burned
everywhere in the gathering dusk, fed by great
logs dragged from Shambhala's devastated forests. The wind carried with it a smell of
woodsmoke and roasting meat. Sangay could
not have said whether it was fear or simple
hunger that made his stomach twist and knot
beneath his ribs.

It was clear to him now, how these invaders
had wrought such havoc in the outer kingdoms, and how they meant to destroy Kalapa.
He gazed with sinking heart at the engines of
war drawn up on the far side of the camp.
Battle-chariots, battering rams, huge boulder-
hurling catapults like toys for giants — all stood
ready for the final assault on the inner lands.

That quick glimpse was enough: hastily he
retreated down the southern slope of the hill
to wait behind a bramble thicket for dark.

He found some crumbs of barley-cake in his
pack, and ate them. He slept for an hour or two.
Then, some time after midnight, he crept back
to the top of the ridge.

The fires were strung out in a long line
across the moraine. The sleeping warriors

sprawled beside them, cocooned in skins and woollen cloaks. At either end of the camp the sentries whistled and paced to keep themselves awake. It was so narrow, that little strip of ground. Sangay could easily have shot an arrow across it. A trifling distance, when he had already come so far. The mountains seemed close enough to touch, and at the same time, as remote as the sacred mountain of Meru, at the centre of the universe.

He longed to be a *lung-gom-pa*, to cross that narrow barrier in an eyeblink, to elude pursuit in a dozen bounds. Or to become invisible, cloaked in magic . . . someday, if he survived, he promised himself, he would master those skills. But for now, he must work with the tools that he had.

Once already, he had made himself as swift as an eagle, light as a windblown cloud. He settled into the lotus position, drew slow breath into his belly, stilled his pounding heart. Time passed. He was calm now, in control of his body: pleasantly warm and properly relaxed. But all the same, depressingly earthbound.

Alone, without Jatsang's voice to guide him, he could not break the iron chains of gravity that held him to the ground.

But he could move across that ground on feet as sure and silent as a leopard's. That too he had learned from Jatsang. And so, sighing, he unfolded himself and got up. Slowly, stealthily, considering every footfall, he made his way down the slope towards the barbarian camp.

The sentries, undisturbed, went on with their doleful whistling. He could hear the soldiers snoring, shifting and turning on the hard ground, groaning in their sleep. Once a sentry cried out and Sangay froze, his belly clenching; but then the man — who perhaps was only calling out a joke to his partner — went back to his pacing, and Sangay began to breathe again.

And then the watch-fires were behind him, and the mountains of crystal and jewelled light opened for him, like the petals of a flower. Their winds grew gentle for him, their passes spread themselves before him, their paths welcomed him. And as the hours — or could it have been days? — went by, the light grew still more vivid, glittering and shimmering and dazzling all about him, as though he were walking through an endless series of prisms. And so he passed through another one of the magic curtains that divide the worlds.

It had been night, and now it was morning. It had been winter, and now was spring. Here the land still flowered. Sangay followed a jade-green river into a wood, misty with new leaves. He walked along the margins of a moon-shaped lake that glittered, in its green depths, with rainbow coloured jewels. On its still surface white lotus flowers grew. Herons waded at the water's edge, kingfishers flashed coloured fire. All the trees — peach, apricot, cherry, persimmon — were a mass of blossom, and musk-deer grazed in their fragrant shade.

He had been walking for a long time. Darkness gathered and the moon rose, a thin silver crescent reflected in the crescent lake. He felt neither hunger nor fatigue. He was buoyant, filled with light, like a *lung-gom-pa*. And then, across the meadows, the darkening hills, he saw a conflagration of golden light burning on the horizon. The glow spread across the dark sky, dimming the moon to a hazy smudge. The grass glimmered yellow beneath his feet.

All his weariness fell away, as though he had
dreamed it. On and on he walked towards the
city that burned like a sacred jewel at Shambhala's
heart.

Book Three

The Dance of the Snow Dragon

KALAPA

Sangay walked all through that night, and with the dawn he came to the outskirts of the city. No farmers, market-bound, trudged the wide roads of Kalapa, no women chattered beside the streams, or gathered fruit in the wild grassy orchards. He could hear the wind in the leaves, birds singing, the faint splash of carp in a temple pond — but no other sound.

Perhaps, thought Sangay, time is counted differently here. Maybe it is their custom to work by night and sleep by day. The streets of Kalapa were wide, tree-lined, empty. The shops and marketplaces were deserted, and from the temples of gold and brass and copper, each set in its own walled garden, no hum of voices, no sound of chanting rose. In the great parks of

Kalapa the crystal-roofed pavilions stood empty, their silk walls fluttering in the wind. No one walked on the long lawns, or gathered hyacinths by the reed-fringed pools, or took the morning sun on the ancient terraces of honey-coloured stone.

Sangay walked on, through that inexplicable silence, until he came to the foot of the hill that rose at the centre of Kalapa. A stone staircase climbed steeply upward. At the top he could see ice-white walls, and golden roofs uplifted like the wings of birds in flight.

Now, within sight of his journey's end, Sangay thought in sudden panic, I am not ready. His clothes were in rags, his pack was empty. Where could he find gifts to honour the King, a white scarf to wear in his presence?

At the foot of the stairs was a stream that fed a little moon-shaped pool. Kneeling, Sangay scrubbed at layers of months-old grime. Then, after he had quenched his thirst, he gathered a handful of lotus flowers as an offering for the King.

At the top of the stairs, encircling the palace, was a glittering palisade of diamond spear-blades. Enormous gates of ebony and brass stood wide as though to welcome him. Within was a white-hot circle of fire.

The flames hissed and spat, a million deadly serpent-tongues lashing at him. In terror, he leaped back.

But he had suffered too much, overcome too many obstacles, to be defeated now. He drew a long breath, and sternly told himself: all experiences are the manifestations of my mind. All sounds are my own sounds. All lights are my own lights. All appearances are illusion. The fire that exists in my own mind cannot burn my flesh.

And as he watched, the flames subsided to a bluish flickering, and he stepped through unscathed.

It was as marvellous as he had dreamed it, this palace of soaring gold-tiled roofs and milk-white marble walls. Carven goddesses danced along the coral mouldings; ornaments of pearls and diamonds tinkled from the eaves. The windows were lapis lazuli, rose-quartz and amethyst, with golden awnings; emeralds and sapphires studded the golden door-frames.

Those doors too stood open and Sangay passed through, into deserted anterooms and corridors and little inner courtyards open to the sky.

In one of these he found a terraced garden where grass grew and a fountain played on glittering stones. Pheasants and peacocks, tame as chickens, crowded at his heels. A gazelle glanced up at him with liquid eyes, and then went peacefully back to its grazing. But elsewhere was emptiness and silence — the silence of high places when snow covers the ground and even the wind is still. No prayer-wheel turned, no gongs and trumpets sounded. There was no bee-hum of chanting, no pattering of feet on stone. No one hurried to greet him, to offer him tea and rice and betel-nut. And no one came to lead him into the presence of the King.

Sangay wandered through a door, a corridor, a courtyard, another door, and presently found himself in a windowless inner hall. Here a forest of pillars, coral and pearl and zebra-stone, supported the graceful golden curve of the roof. Small elegant tables, divans, and brocaded cushions were scattered everywhere. Silk carpets hushed his steps. Embedded in floor and ceiling were rows of crystals, like moonstones, that gave off a soft, diffuse light and a gentle warmth.

Realizing that in this wondrous place no door was closed to him, Sangay felt an immense curiosity, and — in spite of himself — a half-guilty excitement. It was like one of those dreams when the mind is in conscious control and knows that it is asleep: when there is nothing one cannot do, no desire one cannot satisfy. And so, aimlessly exploring, he set off through the maze of passageways that surrounded the central hall.

By now it was long past midday; the slanting sunlight threw shafts of lapis and rose and amethyst across the marble floors. Everything gleamed, glittered, glistened, as though it had just been polished by a ghostly army of novices. But no novices, ghostly or otherwise, appeared.

Presently, looking out through the jewelled windows, Sangay saw the daylight fading, turning to a soft dove-grey. It was the hour of evening prayer. And still the palace slept.

At the end of a passageway he came to an enormous circular room. There was a smell of jasmine, and sandalwood, and camphor. Light poured through glass-covered apertures in the roof.

There in the centre of that rich, silk-carpeted, silk-curtained room stood the gem-encrusted golden throne. Serpents and lotuses twined round it; eight golden lions supported it; half-sitting, half-lying across its seat was a frail old man in the scarlet and turquoise and emerald garments of a king.

When he saw Sangay he braced his hands on the golden arm-rests of his throne and drew himself stiffly upright. The pain in his eyes, in his drawn grey face, betrayed the terrible effort it cost him.

Sangay knelt, and wordlessly offered his bunch of lotus flowers. They were tattered and limp, but the King of Shambhala accepted them as gravely, as graciously as if they had been made of gold.

"At last," said the King, and his voice was a mere flutter of breath in his tense and straining throat. "I feared that the world had forgotten me. I feared that you would never come."

THE DYING KING

At the foot of the Lion Throne an elderly monk in faded robes was turning a prayer wheel. He broke off his mantra to look up at Sangay in puzzled inquiry. "Is it possible?" he said. "A warrior, we were told . . . a hero-knight. But you . . . you are only a boy. Surely you have not come alone?"

Sangay could only nod. What a sad and ridiculous figure he must look — his garments reduced to filthy rags, his hair grown long and straggling, his feet pushing out of the holes in his tattered boots. A hero-knight, indeed . . . he could feel his face growing hot.

"Tell us your name," said the old monk.

"I am Sangay Tenzing. I am a monk of the White Leopard Dzong, in the kingdom of Druk-yul."

"So far," murmured the monk. "And so terrible a journey." He wore the mild, sweet expression of one who dwells apart from the world. "To travel those roads alone . . . "

"For most of the way I had a companion . . ." In some secret corner of his mind Sangay thought, "until she chose to abandon me," but he did not speak those words aloud: " . . . until she chose a different path," he finished instead.

The King shifted in his seat and pressed his hand to his ribs. Though dulled with pain, his eyes, as they met Sangay's, were the eyes of a young man, quick and intelligent. A warrior's eyes, thought Sangay, returning that stricken gaze with awe, and heartsick pity.

The King said simply, "He is the one."

Fingers as brittle and grey as a bundle of dry sticks reached out to Sangay. Gently, Sangay cradled them in his own. Something seemed to pass between Sangay and the King — a fleeting warmth, a tingling shock of energy. It was subtle as breath, as faint as the pulsing of a sparrow's

heart, but Sangay saw the brief easing of pain
in the King's eyes, the sudden surge of hope.
The King said, in his faltering old man's voice,
"There is a curse laid upon Shambhala, and it
is beyond my power to dispel it."

"Your Holiness . . . " Sangay paused awkwardly. How did one address a king? But surely
Shambhala's King was the holiest of men.
"Your Holiness, where are your servants, your
priests, your warriors? Why have they all deserted you?"

It was the monk who replied. "They have not
deserted him. Go into into the kitchens and the
sleeping-chambers, into the guard-rooms and
the royal stables. Go into the houses and temples of the city. There you will find them —
monks and lamas and stable-boys and warriors
alike. For months they have lain in a sleep that
seems halfway to death."

The old monk rose, poured water from a
ewer into a silver cup. He held the cup to the
King's parched lips. Then, returning to his vigil
at his monarch's feet, he went on: "If you have
travelled through the outer kingdoms, then
you have seen how the barbarian army has laid
waste to the land. In Shambhala we have no

experience of war. We have not seen to our defenses. The barbarian leader is a cruel and clever man. With the aid of powerful magicians he built a great road through the snow mountains, and led his army into the lotus kingdoms. And then he put this curse of sleep upon the land."

"And only you were spared?"

"Only I, who by chance was working in the deepest cellar of the palace. Then the barbarian lord sent one of his warriors to the gates of Kalapa disguised as an old beggarwoman. I — who to my eternal shame suspected nothing — opened the gates and let him in. While the King slept, the warrior crept into his bedchamber and thrust a javelin into his side. The wound was cursed by magic, and will not heal. He who had the strength and courage of a leopard, now lies near death."

"Yes," said Sangay, thinking that his heart must break. "And I too know the prophecies, that with the King's death the hordes will overrun Kalapa, robbing the store-rooms of their treasures, destroying the sacred scrolls, so that the wisdom of Shambhala is forever lost to the world. Would you believe me if I told you I had stood in this very room before, in the presence of the King?"

The old monk gave him a startled look. "In vision," Sangay told him. And he spoke of the great dance he had witnessed in this room, the Dance of Gods and Demons. He told of the demon whose cruel teeth tore at the King's throat, and of the eagle that swept down out of the sky to save him.

"Do you know the meaning of your dream, Sangay?" the monk asked.

"Clearly, the lion-demon is the barbarian lord who has stolen the King's strength."

"And the eagle?" the monk asked.

But Sangay shook his head. This time it was the King himself who answered. Raising his head with a terrible effort, he said, "The eagle who wrests it back — you are the eagle, Sangay."

Sangay felt a great weariness come over him, robbing him of energy and will. Surely, he thought, the spell of sleep that has been cast upon the city is affecting me as well.

"I am no warrior," he said. "No hero-knight."

The King's face, as he looked at Sangay, was gentle, and compassionate, and utterly unyielding. For the first time there was a hint of colour in his ashen face, and speech seemed to come more easily to him.

He said, "Why were you able to reach Shambhala — overcoming all obstacles, all temptations — when so many others have lost their way? Why did hidden treasures reveal themselves to you? Why did the crystal mountains and the ring of fire open for you?"

Sangay stood wordless before the King. He had no answer to these questions. All he knew was that he had struggled, and persevered, and that somehow he had won.

"Truly," said the King of Shambhala, "you have learned the lesson of humility. Sangay, it is not the rings of knighthood, the sword and shield and sky-blue robe that makes a warrior. It *is* his humility — and his fearlessness, and compassion, and nobility of spirit. You are the warrior who has the power to break the spell upon Shambhala. It is you who will teach the world the Dance of Gods and Demons. It is you who will give me back my strength."

"Once, a long time ago, before I was a monk, I had another dream," Sangay said. "I dreamed of a demoness whose body stretched the length and breadth of Druk-yul. And I was doing battle with her."

"And in your dream, Sangay, who won that battle?"

"I did," Sangay told him. "I drove dagger-nails into her hair, and her feet and hands, so that she could not move."

"Do you know what that dream meant?"

"No. Only that it frightened me. And that for a long time afterwards I could not put it from my mind."

"You dreamed the future, Sangay. You dreamed of the fate that awaits Druk-yul, if Shambhala is destroyed — if truth, compassion, wisdom are forever lost. And you, Sangay, you dreamed your destiny — you are the one who has been sent to slay the demoness whose limbs are drought, famine, pestilence, war, whose head is selfishness and greed.

"There is a park to the south of the city. It is called Malaya, the Cool Grove. There you will find the Great Mandala, the Wheel of Time."

"Now, Your Holiness?" If only he could rest for a while. If only he could sleep. Though in the past months fatigue had been a constant companion, he had seldom felt such soul-deep, mind-numbing exhaustion. "Must I go at once?"

"At once," said the King. "There is no more time. And remember this, Sangay. The dance is the mandala, and the mandala is the dance. And in the dance is the salvation of Shambhala."

THE WHEEL OF TIME

The old monk brought Sangay tea, a handful of dry cakes, and a torch to light his way.

"Walk south on the Street of White Magnolias, Sangay Tenzing," the monk said. "First you will come to a deer park, and a bridge that crosses a stream; beyond is Malaya, the Cool Grove."

He spoke as a senior monk might address a *gaylong*, courteously, but discouraging argument. Yet as Sangay thanked him, and bowed, and turned to go, he wondered at the look he had seen in the old man's eyes. It was a look of respect, of deference — of something that was close to awe.

Dusk and silence shrouded the empty streets of Kalapa. It was as though the city was holding its breath, waiting for Sangay to shatter the dark spell that enthralled it. That thought weighed heavily upon him, as he went down the steps of the palace, and along the broad leafy thoroughfare leading south.

He found the little painted bridge, crossed the wide deserted lawns of the deer-park, and followed a shadowy path into the sandalwood grove. Mist hung like silken scarves among the branches; the path was lined with orchids, musk-roses, tall feathery clumps of ferns. Somewhere ahead he could hear water splashing over stones.

Presently the trees thinned and Sangay found himself in a clearing, in the midst of which rose a graceful square-sided tower encircled by rose gardens and row upon row of butter-lamps. Covering the near wall of the tower was a mandala, its patterns shadowed and indistinct in the twilight haze.

Sangay struck flint to tinder, set alight his torch and held it high. The rush of flame transformed the dim face of the mandala into a wheel of radiant colour hanging suspended in the dusk. One by one Sangay lit the butter-lamps, until the clearing was filled with flickering points of light.

It was as though he were standing in a temple built for giants, with trees for pillars and the night sky for a roof.

As he gazed at the Great Mandala he saw circles within circles, squares within squares, a bewildering complexity of colour and shape and pattern.

At the innermost heart was the jewelled palace of Shambhala's King. Then came the eight kingdoms of Shambhala, radiating outward like the petals of a lotus; and running through them the four concentric circles of the universe — yellow air, red fire, blue water and dark blue earth. Here too were the seven oceans of the cosmos and the seven rings of golden mountains — circles beyond circles till you came to the farthest reaches of the universe and the outermost ring of fire. Here were gods and goddesses, both wrathful and benevolent; demons and ghosts and demigods, sages and celestial spirits. The black birds of the desert were here, and the dreadful creatures of the night forest, whose jaws dripped blood, and all the monsters of mind and spirit that Sangay had encountered on his journey. And over all, his vast sinuous shape twining in and out of the

pattern, was the Thunder Dragon of Druk-yul,
the great dragon of the snows.

All this — this whirling profusion of gods
and demigods, demons, demonesses, monsters, ghosts, sky spirits — must be patterned,
ordered, interwoven. Like the Mandala itself,
his dance must chart the movements of the sun
and stars and planets, the secrets of time, the
birth and death of worlds, the essence of all
things, from stones and flowers and trees to
men and gods. Somehow the visionary world,
the shapes of dreams, must be given substance.
He must see the dance and the universe as a
seamless whole, from the slow stately opening
steps to the circling, stamping, leaping, spinning frenzy of the final measures.

And when it was finished, when the dancers
in their masks and their jewel-coloured silks
had spun and whirled and trampled and leapt
through the intricate patterns, then the order
of the world would be restored, the sleeping
palace would wake, the wounded King and his
ravaged kingdom would at last be healed.

Why had he, of all the monks in the world,
been chosen? How could anyone imagine he

was worthy of such a task? And yet the King's eyes had held such hope, such trust. . . .

Sangay folded himself into the lotus position and his breathing slowed. Hands on knees, thumb-tips on fingertips, his mind was centred in his middle eye. A slow warmth gathered at the bottom of his spine, a warmth that grew gradually to a burning heat, spreading upward through his body. Deep inside him something trembled, stretched, uncoiled.

He felt a mantra vibrating on his lips. Visions opened within him like the slow unfolding of flowers. He heard strange sounds: a shrill cricket-chirp, a buzzing of cicadas, a flute, a bell. Then came a hollow booming and the roar of distant, fast-moving water. He felt dizzy, and slightly ill. He began to sway from side to side and a vague sense of dread suffocated him. Now he seemed to be in a great soundless space filled with brilliant dots like stars, and radiant shapes, and tongues of flame. And then everything was suffused with a white radiance. And it seemed to Sangay that he stood alone in the still centre of the universe, while all about him whirled the endless and eternal Dance that sprang from the oneness of all things — past, present and future, gods and mortals, dream and reality, the visible and invisible worlds.

Who knows how much time passed, as the world knows time? He became as one with the shapes, the patterns, the intricate figures, the glowing colours of the Great Mandala. A day went by, a night, another day. He felt no hunger, no thirst. His body was an empty husk, abandoned there in the green clearing as his mind reached through the spinning circles of time and space. And slowly, slowly, as water wells up out of a desert spring, as a flower folds back its petals to reveal its heart, he began to visualize the patterns of his dance. What had seemed impossibly complex, became as simple as saying, "The dance is the mandala and the mandala is the dance. I and the dance and the universe are one."

THE GREAT DANCE

To dream a dance and make it real — this was the last and greatest test.

But here was the riddle: who would perform the Dance of Gods and Demons, when all the dancers and musicians of Shambhala lay in a charmed sleep from which the dance alone could wake them?

And as though it had been in his mind all along, the answer came: it was Sangay who had made the dance, now it was Sangay who must invent the dancers.

Out of mind and will, out of moonlight and mist and the darkness of the midnight grove he summoned a troupe of phantom-dancers, lithe and nimble footed in their painted masks and costumes of jewel-coloured silk. These were not

the ragged, flapping ghosts of the wasteland,
born of terror and despair, who had saved him
from the riders. These *tulpa*-dancers were fashioned from all that Sangay had gained on his
journey of wisdom and self-knowledge. He was
their master; it was for him, and for Shambhala,
that they danced. And he called forth musicians, to beat upon the drums, to sound the
thighbone trumpets, to ring the sacred bells.
With swirling scarves and many-coloured silks,
with stamping feet and the rhythmic rapping
of hand-drums, they danced the patterns: the
Five Elements of earth, air, water, fire and
ether; the Five Directions of the World; the Five
Continents of the Universe; the Three Worlds
of Heaven, Earth and Hell. Whirling faster and
faster they danced the endless cycle of death
and birth, the circle of time and the patterns of
all the circling worlds in immeasurable space.

Sangay was sure of his powers now. The
Great Design was as clear in his head as though
it were traced in lines of fire. This was his true
path, the art he had been born to — this intricate ordering of movement, rhythm, colour,
pattern.

He summoned the Demons of the Five Passions — lust, hatred, jealousy, stupidity and pride — and he called the Gods of the Five Wisdoms to do battle with them. He summoned antlered cannibal-demons, ogres, ogresses, animal-headed monsters, fleshless ghosts and all the malignant spirits of mountain and earth and air. And then he created a band of knightly warriors whose pleated robes were the colour of the evening sky.

Day became evening, and faded into night. Higher and higher, ever more wildly the dancers leaped, while the music throbbed and howled, and the stars spun and the planets whirled. At last with a crash of cymbals and a thunder of drums, with piercing war cries and raising of bared swords, the warriors trampled ghosts and demons, vampires and monsters and ogres into the dust beneath their feet. And over all, dark as storm-clouds writhing above the winter peaks, Sangay glimpsed a shadowy uncoiling.

The dance was done. The pattern was completed.

Dazed and exhausted, Sangay woke as from a dream. All around the edges of the clearing he could see the *tulpa*-dancers waiting in their masks and robes and coloured silks. They were quiet as statues now, obedient to his will. For an instant he allowed himself a fierce pride in their creation, and then he remembered what he must do. What Jatsang, in her pride, had failed to do. With sad resolve he spoke a spell of banishment, and like the mists of sunrise they were gone.

But now, in the still air of early morning, Sangay felt a stirring, a shifting, an awakening, as though a cool fresh wind had swept across the sleeping city.

Slowly, stiffly he got to his feet. His garments were soaked with dew, his head throbbed, every joint in his body ached. But beyond the sandalwood grove he could hear the laughter of children, the clatter of hooves along the cobbled streets, bells ringing, a rising hum of prayer. Weariness forgotten, he raced through the wood, through the great park, across the stream; and he saw that the city of Kalapa had woken at last from its enchanted sleep.

MORNING

Sangay saw gardeners weeding the palace gardens and pruning overgrown shrubs, servants sweeping leaves from the walks, grooms leading horses from the palace stables. Both grooms and animals walked stiffly, as though in need of exercise. All the beasts that served humankind, it seemed, had suffered the same enchantment as their masters.

There were rich smells of cinnamon and sandalwood, woodsmoke and lamp-butter, baking bread, meat roasting.

In the corridors of the palace there was a great deal of confused milling about, as everyone from servant-boy to High Lama tried to recall what his business had been when sleep overtook him. Meanwhile the monks, their faces pale and bewildered, set the prayer wheels spinning and picked up the broken threads of ritual.

"Sangay Tenzing, come with me, the King is asking for you." It was the old monk, the King's faithful retainer, his broad, once-doleful face transfigured by joy. Sangay followed him through shining passageways and tall sunlit rooms into the presence of the King.

The King rose at once to greet them. His face looked wan and thin, and he grasped the arm of his throne to support himself. But colour was returning to his face, and his voice had a young man's strength and vigour.

"You have done your work well, Sangay Tenzing," he said. "Now I must do mine."

THE DRAGON WAKES

It was not yet dawn. Through his open window Sangay could hear the moan of trumpets, the insistent clamour of temple bells. The hour had come. From all across the city nobles and dignitaries, lamas, sorcerer-priests and warriors were converging on the great assembly hall in the centre of Kalapa. Sangay snatched up his quiver and bow, hid the phurba under his robe, and ran to join them.

The open-sided hall was ablaze with scarlet and saffron, sky-blue and garnet-coloured silks. The temple bells were silent now. The only sounds were the clicking of prayer wheels, a faint hum of mantras, and now and then the soft, impatient snorting of a horse, its breath making a small puff of smoke in the chill air.

Then out of the morning haze strode the King of Shambhala, leading a tall blue-grey stallion. Beneath its golden trappings, its ceremonial embellishments of white yak tails and rainbow-coloured ribbons, the animal's coat gleamed like rain-wet slate. The King was dressed for battle in a spiked golden helmet and jewel-studded golden breastplate, worn over trousers and coat of brocaded silk. In his belt was a silver-handled sword inlaid with coral and turquoise. All trace of his illness had vanished. What Sangay saw now was a tall, mild-faced, vigorous man in his prime, who wore his authority with ease and grace.

Behind the King came eight High Lamas, each carrying one of the Eight Auspicious Signs: the Treasure Vase, the Endless Knot, the Victorious Banner, the Wheel of Law, the Golden Parasol, the Golden Fish, the White Conch and the Lotus. After them came court musicians, the royal standard-bearers and the palace guard.

Trumpets droned, drums thudded, cymbals crashed. The procession circled the Great Hall and moved slowly out into the city streets. Sangay walked with the other monks, suddenly small and unimportant in that sea of close-cropped heads and russet robes. His voice, as he chanted, joined with a thousand others in the slow, rhythmic ebb and surge of prayer.

They marched along wide avenues lined with flame trees and hibiscus, passed through the city gates and came to a halt on a ridge of high ground overlooking a meadow. Below them the surviving forces of the Eight Lotus Kingdoms were rallying under the banner of their King.

A mingling of hues and patterns like a vast thanka spread out across the field. How like the beginning of a dance it is, thought Sangay, as he watched the colours shift and merge: the ponderous grey shapes of the war elephants, stolid and patient under their embroidered blankets, the sky-blue robes and silver mail of the warrior-monks, the crimson silks of the lamas, the dark-coated ranks of cavalry, bristling with pikes and scimitars and lances. Standards waved and parasols twirled in the chill grey air of morning; prayer-flags and banners fluttered.

For Sangay, it was like a miraculous dream unfolding. He wondered what place in that splendid throng there might be for him, a simple monk untutored in the arts of war. He could not march with the lamas, or the warrior-monks, or the cavalry. But he could follow along behind the magicians. That was his right-ful place, he thought wryly, remembering those long marches at Jatsang's heels.

He found himself staring into faces, and realized, with fleeting sadness, that the face he was seeking was Jatsang's. But that was in an-other lifetime. Like home, like friends and family, like his boyhood, Jatsang belonged to a different world, beyond the wall at the world's end.

Just then one of the King's lieutenants rode down along the ranks.

"Sangay." The sound of his own name startled Sangay out of his reverie.

"His Holiness wishes to speak to you." Dismounting, the man gave the bewildered Sangay a leg up, then swung into the saddle behind him.

"Tell me, Sangay Tenzing, have you any skill with the bow?" The King's face was composed, almost contemplative. He seemed as calm, preparing for battle, as if he proposed to spend the day in prayer.

Sangay nodded — risking, in his confusion, the error of pride.

"I have an abundance of monks," said the King. "What I need are archers. Can you ride?"

Sangay made an ambiguous noise that might have been taken for a "yes". He had ridden yaks, that most unpredictable of beasts. Could a horse be any more difficult?

The King turned to his lieutenant. "See if you can find him a mount."

"But, Your Holiness . . . " Sangay had opened his mouth with no clear idea of how he intended to finish the sentence.

"You will ride with me," said the King, "for who has a better right? Go," he prompted his lieutenant. "If there are no horses to spare, it will do the Chief Abbot small harm to walk."

And so Sangay, dazed with this sudden turn of events, found himself riding to battle at the King's right hand, on a high-spirited white mare with golden stirrups and embroidered reins.

Once again the drums and trumpets sounded, and the army of Shambhala moved off. The day was overcast; a fine silvery vapour clung to woods and fields. Soon they were climbing, through the mist-shrouded foothills, up and up, into ice and cloud. Around them, above them, beneath them, was the pure rock-crystal, colourless and without substance, like frozen air. And suddenly the sun came out, setting alight the frozen streams and waterfalls, the icy cliffs and gorges. They were suspended in the heart of a crystal flower, a great dazzling, amber-coloured jewel.

And then they were over the top of the pass, and descending through a jumble of broken rocks and scree. Beyond lay the bleak wastes of the outer kingdoms, obscured by the smoke of countless fires.

Then came the order to halt. The King, flanked by his lieutenants, rode out onto a rocky spur that afforded a clear view of the lands below. Sangay followed. On the far side of the moraine, massed rank upon rank like a dark stain over the ravaged hills, was the barbarian host. In the merciless light of morning Sangay stared out over a grey sea of armour. He saw the

restless waves of horses in their barbaric antlered masks, the plumed headdresses of the
war-captains, the tall conical iron helmets of
the warriors, the upthrust javelins like stalks of
wheat.

He turned then, to look back at Shambhala's
legions in their robes of scarlet and saffron and
garnet-red. With their silken flags and banners,
their long light bows and wooden-tipped arrows, their slender swords in silver and turquoise sheaths, they were like the embroidered
figures on a temple hanging — a proud ceremonial army, meant to dazzle the eye and uplift
the spirit. But not to do battle with seasoned
warriors. Not to confront this horde of howling
savages, singlemindedly bent on their destruc-
tion.

On this battle's outcome hung not only
Shambhala's riches, her treasure-stores of ancient wisdom, but also the fate of Druk-yul and
all the lands beyond. Who won this battle
would one day rule the world.

As though reading Sangay's thoughts, the
King of Shambhala said softly, "Alas, I fear we
are too few, too ill-prepared." Yet in his face
there was neither fear, nor resignation, nor

despair — only that same look of gentle, meditative calm.

From a thousand throats there rose the sound of chanting, as Shambhala's warriors invoked their gods. It rose, and swelled, and faded, and swelled again, pouring like a river of sound down the rocky slopes. *Om mani padme hum, om mani padme hum* . . . like the great wind that blows between the worlds, it droned and soughed and thrummed and resonated. To Red Tara they prayed, and Black Tara, and the Enemy-Defeating God Dab-tha in his golden mail, and to the old Bon gods of the four directions, to Mother Earth and Father Sky, and all the ancient gods of hill and precipice and valley.

As for the King, he sat like a figure of stone on his motionless steed. His eyes looked inward; it was as though he had ceased to hear, or see, or breathe.

"See," murmured one of the lamas, at Sangay's side. "He has entered the Meditation of the Best of Horses."

Long moments passed. And then abruptly the King roused from his trance, and gave a triumphant shout, and kneed his mount, and

went pounding down the stony track. And all
Shambhala's forces followed.

Sangay looped the reins round the saddle-
horn and crouched over the white mare's neck,
pressing his knees into her sides and clinging
to her mane with both hands. He was conscious
only — in that instant when the first charge
swept him forward — of the wind whipping his
hair and cloak, the electric tingling in his body,
the powerful muscles moving rhythmically beneath him.

And the King of Shambhala rode before
him, his dark hair streaming, his silk robes
billowing out like gold and scarlet wings.

The wind roared in Sangay's ears. The white
mare's hooves danced over the loose stones of
the moraine. Sangay raised his head and risked
a quick glance to the side. It was then he realized that Shambhala's little regiment of holy
men and ceremonial warriors had somehow,
miraculously, become an army.

Where there had been half a hundred war-
elephants, now suddenly there were thousands.
Row upon row of gilded chariots thundered
over the stones. To his left was a whole company
of cavalrymen, their faces painted with red

ochre, their horses bedecked with bright tufts
of feathers, their scaled armour like the leaves
of willow trees. On his right marched an infan-
try battalion, bows slung across backs, chain
mail glinting over padded trousers, black
horsehair plumes waving, lances aflutter with
gaudy pennants. And there, to his rear and
rapidly overtaking the rest, was a legion of
warrior monks on stone-grey stallions, whose
flying hooves seemed barely to touch the
ground.

And in that magical army, marching somewhere at the edge of vision, were all the wrathful gods of dreams and temple paintings: gods
with the heads of tigers, and owls, and wolves,
of lions and crows and cemetery-birds; gods
armed with claws and clubs and dripping fangs,
drinkers of blood and eaters of the dead.

For Sangay, caught up in the midst of it all,
the world was a chaos of lashing hooves and
clanging metal, the serpent-hiss of arrows, the
shrieks of men and horses. Out of that vast
confusion pictures, like dream-images, regis-
tered on his mind: a war-chariot overturned, its
golden wheels spinning, its green silk canopy
in tatters. A High lama, regal in his scarlets,

holding a parasol in one hand, and in the other wielding a long, curving sword. A white yak-tail standard with a broad crimson slash of blood across it. The blank stare of empty eyeholes in a shattered helmet.

And everywhere the grey dust like a choking cloud.

Sangay felt more bewilderment than fear. Most of all he felt a sense of utter futility. The King had said he wanted archers; but what use was Sangay's bow to him now, when he dared not sit upright in the saddle, when he needed both hands to keep his precarious seat?

From the corner of his eye Sangay caught a flash of movement. He jerked his head round in time to see a red-bearded face under a shock of red hair, a raised arm wielding an enormous mace. Grasping the dragon-knife in one hand, the other hand still clutching the white mare's mane, Sangay nudged his mount with his knee, and the animal, as though reading his thoughts, sidestepped as neatly as a dancer. Sangay leaned in, aimed for the vulnerable place in the man's armpit where his oxhide cuirass ended. The thrust had all his weight behind it. He felt the blade bite through cloth and flesh, scrape bone, slither and twist, and then sink home. The mace fell sideways; the horseman shrieked once, and toppled, the *phurba* blade still buried between his ribs. Whether he lived or died, Sangay had no time to find out. In the next instant, another horseman with a javelin was bearing down on him.

Sangay dragged frantically at the white mare's reins and she reared, lashing out with her forehooves. The javelin was aimed straight at her belly.

The man with the javelin grunted, and coughed, and sprawled forward across his horse's neck.

"So, Little Monk," said a voice like a rusty gate-hinge, "you fancy yourself a warrior now!"

She had lost her five-pointed magician's hat, and traded her draggled white shaman's skirt for an infantryman's padded trousers. Her face was smeared with dust and sweat, her hair was chopped short and pulled back with a leather thong. There were splatters of dried blood on her clothes, and a brighter streak of it across her brow; and she was grinning like the first guest to arrive at a wedding feast.

Jatsang put one felt-booted foot on the red-headed man's neck, and wrenched Sangay's *phurba* loose. "Here," she said cheerfully, holding it out.

The two of them were alone on an empty patch of ground, and the barbarian army was in retreat, still raining arrows over the backs of their horses as they fled.

Sangay felt, all at the same time, relief and excitement, and delight in seeing Jatsang again, and unabated terror.

And his arms and thighs and buttocks ached as though he had been riding for a week. Cautiously he slid out of the saddle.

"It is not finished yet," Jatsang said.

He followed her gaze southward, saw the dark line of horsemen cresting the ridge. A kettle drum rolled; the line surged forward. The second charge had begun.

But where was Shambhala's army? Where were the thousands of war-elephants, the battalions of archers, the golden ranks of chariots, the regiments of warrior-monks? Where were the wrathful gods with the heads of beasts? They had vanished, as a dream vanishes in sunlight. A terrible thought came to Sangay.

Had Shambhala's phantom warriors died because the King himself was dead?

All at once the world seemed to shift and tilt. The ground beneath their feet hummed, vibrated. The air shimmered. It was as though, in unseen depths, some invisible thing was rousing, stirring.

There was a slithering, a seething, an immense and serpentine uncoiling. And then, like a sudden gathering of storm clouds, a shadow spread across the field of battle.

Howls of battle-frenzy turned to cries of superstitious fear. Horses shied, reared; the barbarian ranks scattered. Sangay knew if he dared to look up he would see claws as terrible as lightning, scales glistening like the rain on pine trees: a creature whose breath was clouds of fire, whose voice was thunder. Out of dreams, out of legends, out of hidden caverns deep beneath the ice, the Great Dragon of Druk-yul had answered the summons. In the shadow of the Thunder-Bringer, the Dragon of the Snows, Shambhala's King rode forth to reclaim his kingdom.

TULKU

Was Shambhala's ghostly army only a shared illusion, mere shadows against the wall? Or was each one of those warriors a *tulpa*, invested for a time with its own improbable life? It was a riddle to which Sangay might never learn the answer. But what does it matter, he thought, when all things in this world are no more than a waking dream?

In which case, he decided, this victory feast in the Great Palace of Kalapa was one of his more extravagant imaginings. In a walled garden, under the magnolia trees, dozens of low tables and masses of cushions had been set out. Butter-lamps glowed in the branches of the trees, and drifted among the lotus blossoms in the ornamental pool. Incense burners filled the air with fragrant smoke.

It seemed that every dignitary of the Lion Court had been invited, and every lord of the Lotus Kingdoms, and all their female relatives. The women were like flocks of exotic birds in their feast-day silks of lapis and rose-madder, plum and jade and apricot. Amulets and earrings, gold chains and necklaces clattered softly; trellises of lacquered rosewood supported their elaborately plaited hair.

Sangay was beginning to realize, with some dismay, that this feast was in his honour. With so many eyes upon him he felt clumsy and confused, uncertain as to how he should sit or what he should do with his hands. He had drunk too much wine far too quickly, had picked at too many sweetmeats, waiting for the feast to begin. Now he was feeling light-headed, and slightly sick.

At his left elbow sat the wife of the King's First Minister, an ample lady in green brocade with towering gem-encrusted hair. On his right was the King's youngest sister, Yangkyi Kezang, who was lively, and pretty, and no older than Sangay himself. At first she seemed tongue-tied in his presence; but after a while, sensing Sangay's unease was far greater than her own, she chattered her way, like a good hostess, through the unfamiliar courses.

As each new dish arrived she identified it for Sangay: "Honeyed orchids . . . banana-flower buds . . . bamboo shoots in ginger . . . sharks'-fin soup . . . "

She peered with interest at some pale grey-ish slices swimming in sauce. "Pine mush-rooms," she decided.

"I know," said Sangay, ladling some into his bowl. How long had it been since he had tasted that homely dish? He and Dechen had gath-ered them on the forested slopes above the village, and he had carried his proudly home in a basket for his mother to cook. Perhaps it was only excitement, or too much wine, that caused that sudden tightness in his throat, that faint prickling behind his lids.

After the feasting, when the betel nut had gone round in silver boxes, there were singers, accompanied by flute and drum and zither and the seven-stringed *dramnyen*. They sang the lively *Zhe* songs of the warrior-monks, and *Bodra* songs, in the style of Khang-yul, Land of Snows;

and songs which Yangkyi Kezang, who was a scholar, said were written in the ancient language of the Cloud-spirits. There were new songs, too, to celebrate Shambhala's victory, and one, loudly applauded, in honour of Sangay. After that came the dances: the Stag Dance, the Dance of Heroes, the Dance of the Lord of Death. And in the small hours of the night, like a wistful echo from a far-off time, the Drum Dance of Dramitse.

***

It was very late. Yangkyi Kezang and the First Minister's wife had yawned, and brushed the crumbs from their laps, and retired for the night. Darkness seeped into the garden as one by one the butter-lamps winked out.

Just as Sangay, leaning back on his pile of cushions, felt himself sliding into oblivion, there were gongs and trumpets. The King was on his feet, and the High Lamas, and the ministers of the court. And without the least idea of what was happening, Sangay found himself swept along through corridors and passageways in a procession of lamas, dignitaries, knights, court musicians, and a multitude of chanting monks in crested hats.

***

They were in the great chanting-hall of the palace, and it was ablaze with gold and butter-light and polished wood and silken *thankas.* Sangay looked up at the dais. The Chief Oracle was there, in his red robes and lotus-shaped yellow hat, and the Chief Lama in his gold brocade, flanked by a host of astrologer-priests and Superior Monks.

The drums fell silent, the sound of chanting faded, and an expectant hush settled over the room. The Chief Lama stepped forward.

He said, "We have yet to reward you, Sangay Tenzing, for your services to the kingdom of Shambhala. See, we have gathered together many precious things. You may choose for your own whichever ones you wish."

The space in front of the dais was filled with an assortment of objects: drums and flutes, carvings in slate and ivory and rhino horn, a profusion of prayer wheels, jeweled betel nut boxes, a gold and turquoise thunderbolt, a drinking cup made from a human skull, a set of wooden printing blocks, a stuffed catfish, a scimitar, a bell.

Anything in this room? Already he had been amply rewarded — with the King's gratitude, and a place in battle at the King's right hand. Why were they offering him worldly goods, when any raw novice knew that attachment to worldly things was one of the Ten Non-Virtues?

This must be a test, he thought. Was there to be no end to tests, and each one more perplexing than the last?

He said, "Honoured One, I have no need of possessions. I am a wanderer among worlds, and all that I own I must carry with me."

On the face of the Chief Lama was a curious mingling of expressions. It was as though Sangay had, at the same time, given both the right answer and the wrong one.

"Suppose for a moment," said the Chief Lama in a mild and reasonable tone, "that you ceased one day to be a wanderer, a pilgrim. Imagine that you were to possess a house, a store-room, a garden perhaps, an altar for your household gods? In such a case — quite hypothetical, we are both agreed — of all these objects, which would you choose to own?"

Clearly, a polite refusal would not do. A choice was expected. A test. So then. What could he accept without showing covetousness, without being seen to stray from the narrow path of virtue? "Perhaps . . . " he hesitated, thinking hard. For a moment or two he agonized over an ornate jewelled sword, a slender beautifully crafted bow, a zi-stone necklace. But he was no swordsman, and his own bow, though less beautiful, was far more serviceable. And as for the necklace — when could he hope to see his mother, or his little sister, or his cousin Dechen again?

"Perhaps," he ventured, "that prayer wheel. And that slate tablet carved with a mantra . . . and a damaru drum to honour the gods . . . "

The Chief Lama smiled, and shook his head. "Do not choose what you think you are expected to choose, Sangay Tenzing. Choose what seems most familiar to you, out of all these bits and baubles. Choose what calls out to you, 'Sangay, I am yours.' "

A queer test indeed, thought Sangay. But at least he was beginning to understand the rules.

He walked up and down the rows of objects, laid out like temple-offerings on their gold-embroidered cloths. *What calls out to you, 'Sangay, I am yours'.* He remembered a game he and Dechen had invented one day in the yak-pastures. One player hid a stone or a piece of dung, and the other attempted to find it, directed by sly hints and grins and shakings of the head and lifted brows, and sometimes by blind instinct; or — as Dechen insisted — by reading one another's thoughts. Sometimes the stone, the scrap of whatever it was, seemed to guide his movements, drawing him to its hiding place.

What drew him now?

Out of that splendid display, he chose three things:

A small container, a kind of trinket-box, with a broken hinge and half the jewels missing from its lid. A bamboo food-basket, starting to come unravelled. And — after more hesitation — an ordinary set of blacksmith's tongs. He set all these objects down on a small ornate table at the Chief Lama's right hand, and — certain that he had made a complete fool of himself — stood glumly contemplating them.

He realized, after a moment, that no one
was laughing or shaking his head at his
choices. Instead, a murmur of pleasure and
approval went round the room. The Chief
Lama, the court astrologers, the priests and
dignitaries, were nodding and smiling and
looking at Sangay as though he had done
something admirable, and clever, and hoped-
for, and not entirely unexpected.

But what?

"Yak-brained one," said a hoarse and taunt-
ingly familiar voice. The voice spoke, not as he
would have expected, in his ear, but somewhere in the inside of his head. It said, "Is it
possible? Have you still not guessed?"

He turned his head, but there was no one
there.

He realized that the Chief Lama had asked
another question. "Sangay Tenzing, can you
name the objects you have chosen?"

Sangay stared down at the tongs, the basket,
the battered box. And he understood the true
nature of the game he had been playing. Not a
game at all. The drawing back of a curtain. A
revelation.

"His tongs," said Sangay. "He was a black-smith, once."

"His basket. He went out into the forest and gathered mushrooms."

"Pine mushrooms," said the Chief Lama, smiling. "And the box?"

Could it be? Now the last piece of the puzzle dropped into place. "It is the casket from beneath the Burning Lake, that held the secret writings of the gods."

"You have chosen well," said the Chief Lama. And he began to chant:

> . . . *Under the umbrella of three mountains*
> *Like a coiled scarf laid out,*
> *In a pleasant village surrounded by meadow*
> *grass,*
> *Son of Dhondrup and the herdswoman Pema*
> *Drolma*
> *He will be born in the Year of the Iron Horse . . .*

He broke off. "Sangay Tenzing, you were a scholar once. Can you continue?"

Sangay heard his own voice shaping the well-remembered syllables of the *Sangwai Lungten*, the Secret Prophecy of Guru Rimpoche. " . . . *Of dwarf-like stature and red complexion*," he intoned,

"*he will be called Pema . . .*" And with those words
he accepted his place in an unbroken, never-
ending chain of lives.

"You have been attentive to your lessons,"
said the Chief Lama. "Many generations have
come and gone since Pema Lingpa's time, and
not all of his *tulkus*, his earthly incarnations,
have been discovered. But the line of descent
is clear — from Guru Rimpoche and Pema
Lingpa the Treasure-Seeker, to you, Sangay
Tenzing — who from this day will be Sangay
Rimpoche, 'Precious One.' "

After that there were prayers, and invoca-
tions to a thousand gods, and a booming of
horns, and a great wind-storm of chanting.
And finally a crowd of monks surged in upon
Sangay, and caught him up, and bore him away
in triumph in a golden palanquin. And Sangay
realized, when at last they returned him numb
and exhausted and overwrought to his sparse
monk's cell, that since the feast a night had
passed, and a day; and it was night again.

It seemed to Sangay that he would never
sleep again. Even meditation failed him. For
most of his life he had been caught up in great
events, borne along like a blade of grass in a

raging torrent. And now those great events had overwhelmed him.

Sometime after midnight he rose and slipped out of his chamber, wandering aimlessly through the deserted corridors of the palace. At the end of a passageway he discovered a quiet courtyard, full of shadow and starlight. There was a lotus pond and a green canal with a little golden bridge curving over it. And on the bridge stood a tall dark-haired woman, robed in white.

Diamonds glittered at her throat like a string of stars, flashed pale fire from her fingers, hung in dazzling clusters from her ears. Her cropped hair gleamed like a helmet of polished steel.

He knew her at once when she turned towards him, ghost-pale in her garments of snow and frost and starlight. Her face had not changed — that stern, sharp-angled, outlandish face with its slanting, secretive eyes. Though why had he imagined her eyes were black? They were the green of pinewoods, of mountain lakes, of river-jade.

He thought, this must be a sister or a cousin, raised decorously at court while her disreputable twin ran wild in the hills.

But then she laughed — a grunting, coughing, raucous noise that belonged to no one but Jatsang. And all he could do was stare at her in wonder, and delight, and utter bafflement.

"You look like a Cloud-spirit, a *dakini*," he said.

She snorted at that, but all the same he thought she looked pleased. "One does not visit the court of Shambhala in a shaman's rags," she said. And added, when he continued to stare, "All is illusion, Sangay. If I can create a *tulpa*-knight, or thirty fire-demons, I can surely make myself presentable for a feast."

"I did not see you at the feast, Jatsang."

"You had much else on your mind. But I was there. So, it seems my Little Monk is a *tulku*, and I must call him Rimpoche."

Rimpoche. *Tulku.* Hearing them for the first time on Jatsang's lips, he realized the awful significance of those words. From this day forward — for the rest of his life, whatever path he might choose — this was how the world would know him, and how he must learn to know himself. No longer Sangay, the yak-herd; no longer Sangay, the monk; but the sum of all the lives that had gone before him, reaching back and back in an unbroken line through unrecorded and incalculable time. He had imagined such a thing once, in his most secret heart — but one does not expect such imaginings to come true.

Jatsang picked a loose emerald out of the bridge railing and tossed it into the canal. The small splash brought Sangay out of his reverie.

"You were not always so silent, Sangay Rimpoche," Jatsang said.

"I did not always have so many things happen to me, all in the space of a day."

She gave him an odd look.

"To live forever in Shambhala — what greater blessing could anyone ask? To be honoured as a hero, the saviour of the kingdom and the living incarnation of a saint? Have you not reached your journey's end, Sangay? Is this not the perfect happiness that all men seek?"

For Sangay, these were no idle musings, but questions to which — today, or tomorrow, or one day soon — he must find an answer.

He thought of Kalapa's lush green meadows, her pleasure-gardens and pavilions, her flowering woods. He imagined how it would be to live in a place where the fruit was always ripe upon the vine, and the grain in every season ready for the harvest. He imagined a life of ease, and happiness, and the company of those who, while immeasurably wiser than he, still respected him for his wisdom. A place where no one knew that he had ever been clumsy, or wilfully disobedient, or a fool. And for one instant there rose unbidden the lively intelligent face of Yangkyi Kezang.

He said, "I have travelled far, endured much, to reach Shambhala, and it is everything I dreamed of."

"And yet?"

"And yet there is something gnawing at me, that will not let me be content."

"It is the road you have not yet travelled," Jatsang said. There was compassion in her voice, an unexpected gentleness. Had those qualities been there all along, Sangay wondered, and he too immersed in his own affairs to see them? And there was something else, deeper and more fiercely hidden . . . it came to him, finally, with a shock of surprise. She too can be hurt, he thought. She too fears loneliness, and the grief of parting.

***

For nine days he meditated, and no answer came to him, and he was near to despair. On the tenth night, in the darkness of his cell, he thought he heard the sound of breathing, and saw in the grey rectangle of the doorway a hunched and hooded figure. It was no greater in stature than a child, but squat and stooped and shuffling, as though cursed in the womb by some strange deformity. In one hand the figure held a basket, in the other a pair of blacksmith's tongs.

Sangay felt no trace of fear. Nor was he surprised at this visitation. They had, after all, but a single soul between them.

"There will be no rest for either of us," said his ghostly visitor, "until you make up your mind what you want." His was not a scholar's voice but a peasant's — rough-edged, plain-speaking, a little impatient, as though he had business elsewhere needing his attention.

"Help me, Holy One. I have struggled with this question for nine days and nine nights, and am no nearer a decision."

"So then . . . I will tell you four things," said Pema Lingpa, "and you can make of them what you will. First, that the scholar does not acquire wisdom for its own sake, but for the sake of sharing it with others. Second, that the Treasure-Seeker does not seek out treasure for its own sake, but for the good it will do others. Third, that the dancer cannot see the pattern of the dance."

"And the fourth?"

Pema Lingpa said, "That there are two parts to every journey. There is the outward journey, and the journey home."

And then the hooded shape thinned and faded, like smoke upon the air. And the doorway stood dark and empty as before.

***

In the southern distance Shambhala's peaks gleamed white as milk against a sky of flawless sapphire. Sangay settled his pack against his shoulders. It was a perfect day for travelling.

"Once," he said to Jatsang, "I asked if you would teach me magic."

"And what did I say?"

He smiled. "As I recall, that you would teach me magic if I learned to walk naked in a winter gale, and bathe in frozen rivers, and sit on a mountaintop all winter in a wet sheet."

"And will you?"

"If I must."

She gave a howl of delighted laughter.

"So you would, Sangay Rimpoche," she said. "So you would. You would complain, and trip over your own feet, but still you would do whatever I asked."

"And you would teach me to be a *lung-gom-pa*? You would teach me *tumo*?"

"Oh, Sangay Tenzing, I will teach you anything you wish. But to far-travel, mind-speak, to make a fire in the belly — those are little magics. Yours is the great magic. You have seen the gods dance. It is not I who am your master, but the one whose spirit your body clothes."

Sangay thought of the long journey over the high passes, the rivers that must be crossed, the deserts of black glass and demon-haunted forests.

But he was wiser now. He had seen the monsters that lurked beside the path and knew them for what they were. "I have a destination," he told Jatsang, smiling. "Now I must discover the true path that leads there."

"That road is long," Jatsang replied. "The passes are bitter cold in winter. Shall I come with you, Little Monk?"

"But how shall I keep pace with you?" he asked.

"I can run with the wind when it suits me," she said. In her voice he heard laughter, and self-mockery — and gladness. "Maybe now it suits me to stump along like a three-legged dog."

And without looking back to see whether Sangay followed, she set out at a brisk lope across the plain.